Love Lives Forever

Love Lives Forever

EVERYBODY WANTS TO FIND TRUE LOVE,
BUT EVERY FAMILY HAS THEIR OWN SECRETS.
THE TIPO FAMILY HAS A FEW EXTRA.

A Novel Series by

Ayla Jimenez

AuthorHouse™
1663 Liberty Drive
Bloomington, IN 47403
www.authorhouse.com
Phone: 1-800-839-8640

© © 2012 by Ayla Jimenez. All rights reserved.

No part of this book may be reproduced, stored in a retrieval system, or transmitted by any means without the written permission of the author.

Published by AuthorHouse 5/2/2012

ISBN: 978-1-4685-3588-4 (sc)
ISBN: 978-1-4685-3587-7 (hc)
ISBN: 978-1-4685-3589-1 (ebk)

Library of Congress Control Number: 2011963464

This book is printed on acid-free paper.

Because of the dynamic nature of the Internet, any web addresses or links contained in this book may have changed since publication and may no longer be valid. The views expressed in this work are solely those of the author and do not necessarily reflect the views of the publisher, and the publisher hereby disclaims any responsibility for them.

To everybody who believed in me,

especially Justin Cain

Thank you

Prologue

Marcus Tipo was leader of the clans, and now it was time for him to choose his next bride. Noticing a long blond haired woman from across the room, he choose her. Her name was Allision, a guardian. That night they we married. But soon their ceremony was cut off short, due to a guard running in the castle's door. Bowing quickly than standing, still trying to catch his breath, the guard managed to speak. "My lord, sorry for my intrusion, but it's the Veach clan, they've all gone rouge!"

Without hesitation every guard followed Marcus to the Veach castle. Inside, there was yells and screams of fear, no doubt from the maids. As Marcus entered, with Allision following behind him, there was blood everywhere, bodies mangled into pieces.

Marcus quickly threw the candles on the castle's floors as the smell of fresh burnt blood filled the air. Walking out, Allision heard a babies cry, disregarding Marcus's orders to stay, Allision ran up the spiral of stairs with Marcus on her every move. She followed the cries until she came to a room, with two baby cribs. One was empty while the other had a baby boy inside crying. Picking up the baby Allision looked into his eyes, light brown, he was not yet a rouge.

Smoke filling the castle Marcus led Allision out of the castle while she was cradling the little baby boy, who to Allision only looked to be a year old. Leaving the castle, standing back, Marcus and Allision watched as it went up in flames. Quickly hearing another babies cry, Allision handed the baby boy to Marcus, who was yelling at her telling her to stop but without obeying his orders, Allision did stop. Slowly, the cries began to fade away until there was nothing left but the burning of the wood from the castle, it was too late.

Returning to the Tipo castle Marcus and Allision left the child with the maids and the guard with strict orders to have him raised to be a guard, without knowing about what has happened. Doing so Marcus also ordered that they removed the Veach name and give him a new a name. After the night settled, Marcus and Allision left, not to be seen again.

~17 YEARS LATER~

Part One

Chapter 1

"No one in the world knows how werewolves came to be, the World doesn't even know they exist, but I do. It was the night before my 16th birthday and as I was dreaming I was running through this forest, the trees arched over each other which blocked the sun, fog falling on the ground. Then out of nowhere this man appeared, just standing there, with a long finger pointed towards me he said "It is your time now." He said with a deep creepy voice.

I woke up to the blazing, not to mention annoying sound to my alarm clock. 7 am, time to get ready for school. After my shower I was blowing drying my long blond hair, but the thought of the dream never left my mind."

The vibrating noise from Kathern's phone startled her. "Happy birthday girl, see ya @ skool xo Jai." Jai Manks has been Kathern's best friend since preschool.

Running down the stairs to grab a pop tart and get on the bus, but to Kathern's surprise her parents was sitting at the table, together, quiet. Weird to Kathern because her father works over nights at a factory and her mother was lawyer, to Kathern something wasn't right. There was a weird silence, something that never happened. Trying to avoid the awkwardness Kathern grabbed her food and her clutch and started heading out the door.

"Happy birthday Kate." The voice came from Kathern's mother, sounding serious.

"Thanks." Was all Kate could manage out. The dream still lingering in her mind.

"You had it, didn't you? You had the dream." Kate's father, Marcus, sat straight up, hands cupping together on the table.

"It was just a dream dad, besides I'm late for school. Bye." "That can wait, this however, cannot. There is something we need to explain to you. Now that you are 16, it's your time now." That last sentence sent shivers down Kate's spine. The same as her dream. "What are you talking about?" Kate looked at both of them, neither one blinking or moving. It almost seemed like they weren't even breathing. What was going on? They all three stayed that way for what felt like an eternity to Kate.

"Sit down honey." The voice from her mother startled her, but she did as she was told. Then Marcus pulled out a huge book that to Kate looked to be at least a hundred years old. The 'words' on the cover was from a completely different language, but somehow looked familiar. "This is the 'Book of the Blood Moon' and now that you are of age, and had the dream, it's time to explain. Marcus slid the book across the table to Kate, she barely touched it, but these, these visions appeared about wolves. Scared to death Kate quickly pulled back her hand. Kate managed to look at her parents to say "Explain what?" both of her parents looked at each other, then her mother cleared her thought as a gesture for Marcus to speak.

"Your name is Kathern Tipo, from the Tipo clan. Usually the dream appears when you turn 13, but since you are half . . ."

"Half what? And what the hell is this talk about clans?" her mother looked at her with a looked that meant watch your mouth and listen at the same time. Kate sank in her chair, hands crossing each other in her lap, her eyes never leaving the book.

"My name is Marcus Tipo, I am the leader of the clan Tipo, and you my dear are a princess, a lycan princess."

A headache stirred in Kate's head, she wasn't much of a morning person anyways and this wasn't making any matters better. But this was too much for her to handle right now "A what?!"

"A lycan, Kate, you, like me are lycans, shape shifters, werewolves to be more precise."

"Since you are only half lycan your dream came last night, at midnight, the moment you turned 16. Your mother is not a lycan, no, but she is something else."

"Like WHAT?! What could be worse than this?" Kate's breathing was starting to get heavier and heavier with ever word.

"I am a guardian, with the powers of water. I met your father 17 years ago. I was sent from another tribe to guard him, to protect him, but to our surprise and everybody else's we fell in love, and left. You are half lycan; however you are also half guardian to water." Kate was shocked, could hardly breathe, what was she hearing? She has always had this fascination with wolves and when she was in water she somehow felt calm, relaxed. All of this was too much for Kate to handle, she almost couldn't believe it. She looked back down at the book, discussed she didn't even want to touch it; however something inside her told her to open it. When she did there were those 'words' all over the pages, as she flipped through the book a picture caught her eye. It was the forest, the one she was running down in her dream, except in the middle there wasn't a man, no it was a wolf.

"I had a dream last night, with this image, except for the wolf, it wasn't a wolf, it was a man." Kate pointed to the picture and then looked at her father. "What's going to happen now?" Kate asked, even though she did not want to hear the answer.

"Since you are only half lycan, and a female lycan at that, you can shape shift whenever you like, not just under the full moon like male lycans. However in order to receive your powers you must change under the blood moon, which happens to be tonight, as for you water powers you can control and use them whenever you like." Marcus explained. Kate never saw her father look so serious, and she was starting to get scared. *'What the hell am I?'* she asked herself.

"This book will help you learn everything you need to know about lycans and guardians. The words will come to you and start to make sense once you transform the first time. You will then learn the language of the lycans. After you change tonight we must go to the clan, for your acceptance."

"And if I choose not to change? What then?" Marcus's eyes turned pitch black unlike anything Kate has ever seen.

"Then the clan will die off. You are a princess Kate, and soon you will be queen of the clan Tipo. Your mother's powers will come, when you least expect it, they are controlled by your emotions. So choose, Princess."

Kate looked up at him again, this time with fear rushing through her body. "And what about school?"

"You may finish your high school year if you wish, but then we must return to the clan regardless otherwise. You may also miss school today if you wish ... but that would be a shame." A slight smile fell upon Marcus's face. In confusion Kate looked at him. "Why dad?" "Well, seeing how it is your 16th birthday, I wouldn't want this to go to waste." He threw her a set of keys. *Great finding out I am a lycan princess and he gives he a car?* She kept her thoughts to herself, but did say thank you and walked out the door.

"Kate, you might want to take this, look it over, things might come to you." Allision handed her the book. "Thanks, bye." Kate walked out the door and there was a black conversable car.

"Marcus, this might not be a good idea, if we would have waited . . ."

Marcus cut her off, "Listen Allision, one way or another she was going to find out. Let's leave it at that."

Chapter 2

As Kate was driving to school, all she could think about was what was just told to her, everything has been a lie. Kate passed the school and drove to the city park. She found a tree to sit under, with a lot of shade. She looked around to make sure nobody was around and pulled out the book. Looking over the cover the 'words' slowly seemed to make sense just not completely too where Kate could understand. She sat there scamming over the book, looking at the pictures, trying to make out the sentences, but still nothing. Some of the drawings however seemed familiar, from her dreams. She looked at her cell phone and realized three hours has gone by. Kate had a choice to make, by tonight, a choice that would change her life forever. Thinking, thinking hard she has made her decision. Kate gathered her belongings and jumped in her car. Driving home she hoped this was the right decision.

Once again, she was surprised to see her parents sitting in the same spot almost unmoved. "Is it going to hurt?" Kate asked her father, with fear in her eyes. "Am I going to have to eat . . . animals . . . people?" her father laughed at her questions

"No, once when you transform you can be a lycan for as long as you like. But sometimes, in the woods, a fox or a deer would be your only means of survival. Other than that you may act as if nothing has changed, live a partly normal life. However the first changes hurt but that will fade away as your body gets uses to the changes. Even in your lycan form you may still use your water powers."

Looking shocked, looking at her mother, Kate was scared. The words barley made it out of her mouth . . . "When do we do it?" Her father turned to look at her mother, and then turned back to Kate, "Tonight, at 11, you will meet us outside." Kate started for her room. "Marcus, we both know this is not what she wants, she wants a normal life." "Allision, this is the only way."

Kate sat down on her bed, looking over the book once more and still nothing made sense to her. She sat the book down by her bed, set her alarm for 15 till 11 and laid down, despite all that was going on in her mind, Kate managed to fall asleep.

The blaring sound of the alarm clock woke Kate up almost instantly.

She quickly put on her shoes and tied her hair in a bun. She met her parents outside in their back yard, which to Kate almost seemed perfect Their back yard was closed in with a long tall wooden fence, surrounded by big tall trees. Butterflies flew in Kate's stomach when her gaze met that of her fathers, King Marcus Tipo she thought. Kate walked up to him and met him face to face, "What now, dad?"

Marcus waited for a moment fixed on her bright blue eyes. He gazed at her and then looked up at the moon, turning a deep crimson hue color, the blood moon she thought. Marcus's gazed returned to hers. "Relax my child, let the feeling of the moon take you in, feel it, let it become you." Her mother stood in the corner away from Kate and Marcus, watching. Kate closed her eyes, thought about the moon, the blood color of it, then out of nowhere she felt a deep tingle in her stomach, not butterflies, no, but more relaxing. When Kate opened her eyes and looked around. To Kate it seemed like somebody turned on a light, everything seemed brighter and alive more than ever, the trees glowed. Looking down she saw paws, *'Did this really just happen? Can this happen?' 'Yes my child, it can and it did'* Nobody spoke but she recognized the voice almost instantly, it was her father's voice. Kate looked to the left of her and saw a big dark black wolf, with dark eyes, the same way her father's eyes looked earlier this morning. *'Can I talk?' 'No you cannot. However lycans share a telepathy connection with each other, that is how we are talking now.'* She looked down at her paws again, HER paws. She turned back to the black wolf, her father, *'What now dad?' 'We wait a few more minutes, let your new form get used to the way you are, in a away trying to get a hang of it. I will be right behind you. I promise, nothing bad will happen.'*

She looked around the yard then her gaze returned to her mothers, their eyes meeting. Kate strolled over to her. Her mother bent down, crying, Kate rubbed against her, hoping to let her know she's ok. *'She knows,'* Marcus said behind Kate, *'Look at yourself Kathern.'* Kate turned around and looked inside the glass sliding doors. There was a huge black wolf, her father. However next to him was a much smaller wolf, white with sky blue eyes, that was her. Every spot on her body was white, except for a pitch black spot on her tail. Like father like daughter she thought. Kate continued to walk around the yard, the flowers all seemed brighter, grass glowing a green unlike anything Kate has ever seen before. She returned to her father, eyes meeting once again, *'So how do we change back?'* Marcus turned and looked at Allision, and then she went inside. She came back out a few moments later carrying two blankets. Marcus turned to look at his daughter, how beautiful she looked, he knew he couldn't show it but he was smiling with delight, the Tipo clan will continue one more generation, with a pure white as its leader. He looked at Kate, eyes meeting, *'Just as you thought of the moon, think about yourself as you were before.'*

    Kate looked at him, looked up at the moon one more time, and then looked down. Kate closed her eyes thinking about her body as it was before, furless, tailless. Then she had the same tingling feeling in her stomach again, like a pleasure, then without even knowing it, she was down on her hand and knees, screaming out in pain, crying. Her whole body burned all the way down to her bones, aching. Her mother ran up to her and wrapped the blanket around her, holding her in her arms. Marcus stood next to Kate, wrapped in the other blanket. He knelled beside them, "In all of the Tipo clan there has never been a Pure White lycan. I am proud of you, Princess Kathern."

    Her mother grabbed her and helped her up to her room. Kate got dress and laid down in her bed. "Honey, I am so sorry we didn't tell before, but now you embraced the powers, it will get easier. As for your water powers they will develop soon, once they do I will be here to help you. Even in your lycan form, you can control water. All it takes is practice." Allision looked at her daughter proud.

    "Mom," Kate looked up, pain still pushing through her body, but worst, her mother could see it in her eyes. "Why hasn't there ever been a Pure White wolf before?"

    Allision sat down nest to Kate, rubbing her hair out of her eyes, "Because honey the legends are said only a true lycan with special powers can be pure white. Read the book, now everything will make sense." Allision kissed Kate on her forehead, and left the room. Still in pain, Kate picked up the book and started reading.

Chapter 3

For the rest of the week Kate took a family leave from school, inside she felt like a freak. But in the meantime Kate tried to work on her water powers with her mother, her father always outside watching her practice, he made her feel like she had to get it right, she had to do better no matter how hard she was trying. There was three buckets of water in the far end of the yard, while Kate, Allision, and Marcus was back by the sliding doors.

"Ok Kate, focus on one bucket at a time, picture, visualized the water inside the bucket, try to bring it out of the bucket." Kate did as she was told, visualizing the water, thinking, but nothing happened. Getting frustrated she tried again, and to her disappointment, nothing again. Furious she turned around and started yelling "Cant we stop now?! I have changed every night and all day I am out here with these stupid buckets of water and not even a single drop has moved! Can we quit now please?" Her eyes glowing a deep blue, but her parents did not move their gazed from the buckets. "What? What now? What did . . . ?" As Kate turned around, the water from all three buckets rose, forming on ball of water. All three of the stood there in shock.

Kate leaped with joy "I did it, mom, dad, I did it!" Then to their surprise, the water ball dropped as did the smile on Kate's face. "I'll be in my room if anybody needs me." Kate ran inside and went to her room.

What's wrong with me? Why can't I do this? Kate had million thoughts going through her head. She picked up the book and started reading.

She didn't understand, before these 'words' was just marking, but now they made out works she could read. She read about guardians, how they are not guardians how we thinks but friends to lycans, protectors. Guardians help lycans learned their ways, help them discover their powers. She read about the clans of the lycans, the Tipo clan was the leading clan. She looked through the guardians clans but something stuck out to her, a name, the Manks clan. Jai Manks, could it be a conscience, or . . . was Jai a guardian? Full of more questions, she kept on reading, according to the book even guardians have the power to use telepathy. Wanting more answers, she laid the book down on her dresser, thinking, and then an idea popped in her head. Turning off her desk light, she laid down and went to sleep.

Kate's alarm went off the next morning, and she did as usual, took her shower, braided her hair, grabbed her clutch, and ran out the door. She drove herself to school, waiting for Jai. As she was thinking, Jai was only a couple of months older than her; could she really be . . . a guardian? Kate had the biggest smile on her face once when she saw Jai. They ran up to each other.

"Oh my god, where on earth have you been Kate? I've been texting and calling you all week." Jai said with a little worry in her voice. Trying to keep her mind clear, Kate replied, "Oh, I just had some family . . . issues to deal with." She gave Jai a fake but convincing smile. With a smile in return Jai replied "Oh, well that's cool, I took extra notes for you. Here" As Kate reached out to take the notes she thought to herself, hoping Jai wouldn't 'hear' her. *'I just found out I am a lycan princess, Jai'*

Immediately Jai dropped the papers, but Kate got the answer she really didn't want. "Um . . . um . . . Oh my I dropped the notes, I'll pick them up." Nervously Jai bent down to gather the notes, Kate joined her thinking again *'I know what you are, Jai, you are a guardian, what do you specialize in?'* Jai stopped and looked in Kate's eyes. Jai's eyes turned red, almost blazing, like fire. Instantly Kate knew it was fire that Jai specialized in.

"I got to go, see you later Jai." Kate grabbed her things and ran to her car. Driving home she couldn't believe what had just happened, her best friend for years was a fire guardian. How many more of us, of them are out there? Storming in her house, nobody was there, everybody must have gotten back to their 'normal' lives.

Anger, confusion, pain, disappointment, everything was bubbling inside her. Next thing Kate knew she heard the pipes rattling and the kitchen sink blew up, water flowing everywhere, spreading all around the kitchen. Yelling "Stop, just STOP!" And just like that they did. Anger, that's what controls her powers. Her father did say that her powers would come from her emotions. Without either parent home she went to the backyard, without the pressure from them she thought she could it out her powers alone. She grabbed a blanket and an extra change of clothes. Kate quickly ran outside and filled the three buckets with water. First she thought shape shifting, she closed her eyes, imagined the blood color moon and felt the tingling, it was happening. She opened her eyes and looked around, looked down and saw the paws *'YES!'* she thought. Looking at the fence, she wondered how high she could jump. Running quickly towards the fence she jumped but only to hit the middle of the fence. She had hurt her left paw, limping to the blanket she thought of her human form, when she opened her eyes she was herself, naked. She quickly got dressed and thought now it was time for the water.

Chapter 4

𝒦ate was still outside practicing with the buckets. She was able to get one bucket of water to rise into a bubble, then slowly dropped it back in the same bucket, both of her parents without her knowing, was watching her from one of the windows.

"She's getting used to this, Mark." Allision said, hugging her husband. "Yeah, she is but we both know soon it will be time to return to the clan." Marcus held his beloved wife even harder, then to her surprise he led her upstairs to the room.

Meanwhile, outside Kate was focusing on two buckets now, but something caught her eye, along with her new sense of smell. In the corner of the fence was something, somebody, her heightened sight made it that much easier to make out who, or what it was, another lycan. She quickly transformed and ran over to him. She could tell it was a male by her sense. His eyes were a jade green color and his fur was a light tan brown color. The stranger bowed his head, '*Princess Tipo, I see you've learned the secrets of the clan. I have a message for your father. You, your father and your mother are requested at the Tipo castle, as soon as possible.*' He bowed his head once again, Kate looked at him in amusement, how beautiful he was. Quickly she looked at him, '*Consider the message sent.*' The male wolf bowed his head once more, then just disappeared. Kate never knew that could happen, it was never mentioned in the book. To Kate, she had a lot more to learn.

She turned her head towards the house, wondering how far telepathy could travel, she called for her father. Within minutes he was outside, her mother as well with a blanket. Kate tried to run but remembering the pain in her paw made her limp, in pain she limped over to her mother who wrapped her in a blanket as she transformed back to her human form.

"Dad there . . ." Marcus cut her off before she could say anything else. "I know Kate, I heard the message. It's time we pack." Marcus said, then swiftly he went inside the house. With her mother by her side, Kate regained her strength and pulled herself to her feet, her left hand starting to bruise. Allision looked at her with a questioning look, but before she asked Kate said "Don't ask mom, training accident, that's all. Where exactly are we going?"

"Alaska?! Why Alaska? It's so cold there." Kate couldn't believe they had to go all the way to Alaska. "It's cold and it is also isolated, that's why lycans can with stand the cold weather." Marcus's words were so deep as in don't ask any more questions.

They soon boarded the plane but all Kate could think about was Jai, and the unknown stranger. Who was he? All the thoughts ran through her head, but slowly Kate started to drift to sleep. Eleven hours later they were in a van driving on some deep back roads in Alaska. Looking around the road looked strangely familiar, the road, the tress, the way they arched. Then it hit her, the road was the same road from her dream, from the book. That's where she saw this before. At the end of the road was a long, wide black gate surrounded by three guards on each side, Kate could sense they were lycans as well.

The biggest guard came to the van window, and with a surprised look he said "Lord Tipo, welcome home." Home, Kate thought, this was not her home. Within minutes they were walking up to the stairs that lead to the castles main doors. The castle was big, with towers surrounding it. Over the main doors were the words "TIPO CASLTE"

Chapter 5

*W*alking around the castle, with everybody bowing to her, made Kate feel uncomfortable. One guard bowed his head and said "Hello Princess Tipo, how are you?" disregarding the guard's question Kate just kept on walking. She walked all the way up the stairs to find her 'room'. She didn't feel at least at home, she wanted to go back to Minnesota, quiet Minnesota, with her friends. She made her way to her room and started to unpack until there was a knock on her door. "Princess, your dinner." A young man, maybe a year or two older than Kate was holding a gold tray. Grabbing the tray and about to shut the door, Kate turned around and looked at the young man once more. Jade green eyes, light tan hair, light skinned, to Kate he looked so familiar. Knowing he was a lycan as well made Kate want him even more. A slight smile appeared on the young man's face, '*Shit*' Kate thought, feeling a rush of heat to her face, she quickly then said thank you and shut the door.

Tired from the flight and the drive here along with having her stomach full, which Kate was hoping was roast beef, Kate laid down and fell asleep almost instantly. When Kate woke up the next morning she started to get dressed until something caught her eye. There was an owl at her window, something about it wasn't right. It was a tan colored owl, but that wasn't what surprised Kate, the tips of the owls feathers were red, like fire, blending together almost like flames. As Kate started to walk closer to the owl, it flapped its wings and was gone. Thinking it was nothing Kate threw the thought out of the mind, there was enough weird stuff going on anyways.

Kate sat down on the bed and pulled out the book, looking it over.

She learned a lot about these powers that lycans can posses. There are many different types of powers, even guardians can posse powers, but for lycans and guardians they usually only posse one certain power.

Reading over the book she found out that the clans formed in 1437. At first there was 15 clans that started, but some went rouge and had to be killed, others did the same and now there was only six remaining clans, but right now during our time the clan Veach is going rouge, other than that there was Clan Tipo, Clan Hagen, Clan Taylors, Clan Spradlin, and Clan Forestry. Rouge, does that mean that they are evil, Kate thought to herself.

"Yes, my dear." Kate jumped to the voice and startling presence from her father. "Good morning dad, how's mom?" Kate looked at him but he seemed very serious, something in his eyes gave Kate a turning feeling in her stomach. "Today is the day the Clan will accept you as their princess. We will be throwing a ball in your honor and the other four remaining clans will be here. Then, my dear, you will have to pick a suitor." Marcus's gaze never left Kate's.

"A what?!" Kate asked, her voice loud and echoing through her overly large size room, but deep down she already knew the answer. Her father's gaze staring upon her made Kate feel even more frightened. "A suitor, a prince, to wed and well reproduce. I understand that this is all a bit early and hard for you to fully grasp the concept, however Kate if you do not choose a suitor tonight, we will choose one for you by the end of tomorrow night."

"What the hell?! I'm suppose to choose a complete stranger, marry him and pop out kids? Dad I . . ." With the raise of his hand Kate stopped talking instantly. "No, you will be courted for two years, guarded, and then once when you are married, yes, you are to keep the blood line going make a new generation." Royalty or not, that was not going to happen to Kate.

"And if I say no?" Kate asked with a little bit of sarcasm in her voice. Her father's gaze stood even deeper, eyes turning pitch black. "There is no other choice. Your mother will take you into town to pick out your dress. Understand Kathern?" Scared Kate nodded her head. Just as he appeared, Marcus disappeared. Kate laid back down on her bed, tears forming in her eyes. How can they do this to me? Pawn me of like a damn animal? Kate's thoughts made her wanted to cry even more. Hearing a knock on her door, she looked in her mirror and she realized that she did look upset, quickly wiping her eyes, realizing that that wasn't going to help, her future was already chosen for her. When she opened the door, it was the young man from last night, carrying another plat of food. "Your breakfast, Princess." He reached out the tray and bowed his head. She grabbed the tray and said thank you. As she was shutting the door, the stranger spoke, "Is there something troubling you Princess?" Kate was indeed upset but she didn't want anybody to know. "No, I'm fine, and please call me Kate." She reached out to shake hands but all the young man did was bowed his head on last time. "Chris, Chris Goshen, I'm one of the guards, in training." Chris, Kate thought what a nice name.

"Thank you Princess . . . I mean Kate." Chris looked at her and smiled. With delight she smiled back and shut the door. But she still felt his presence there, his scent. She had smelt it before, but now . . . now it was gone, he was no longer there. There was something about Chris but Kate couldn't figure it out, something special. Within 30 minutes Allision walked into Kate's room. "Ready?" Allision looked at Kate staring out the window. Kate didn't say a word, she only got up from the window and walked out the door, with her mother following her. The drive to town seemed to take forever but finally they reached the stores. Allision parked near the side walk and both ladies got out of the van. They walked around until they reached a formal dress store called 'Formally You', what a name for a dress store Kate thought. They entered the store and looked at many dresses but didn't one pleased Kate, until she saw a green dress. Kate tried it on and much to her surprise it seemed to fit her perfectly, hugging every curve of her body, like it was made just for her. There was a slight slit up the right side, just barely above her knee. There was only one strap on the left side, instantly Kate fell in love with the dress, and the color, it almost reminded her of Chris's eyes.

"This one mom, this is the one I want, please?" "of course my dear." Allision walked up to the store worker, whispered something in her ear and with an understanding nod, the lady left. Kate was admiring the dress, thinking about Chris. The store lady returned with a box, once when she opened it, the box reveled a shawl, the same color as the dress. Kate took off the dress and when they went to the register Allision simply said their names and without asking for a dime the lady smiled and handed Allision their belongings. Walking around town they passed many different stores, picking up a few more things for Kate's ball. A pair of silver heels, a silver pin for her hair, and a little bit of make-up.

Ayla Jimenez

On their walk back to the van, Kate looked at her mother, with questions storming in her mind, and before she could control herself the question just popped out. "You and dad never met at a store did you? You was handed off by your parents, just like what you're doing to me. Right? Tell me I'm right mom!" Allision kept on walking but then stopped and turned around to look Kate in her eyes directly. "Yes Kate, that's how it happened. We didn't like each other at first, but within the time we had, we learned to respect each other, then that respect turned to likeness, and soon that turned to love. When I had you, we feel even more in love. And that's where it started, trust me honey," Allision cupped her hands on Kate's face "It might not be what you want it to be, but it might not be what you expect." Allision kissed Kate's forehead. They continued to walk to the van. Those words rung in her head, her heart, and before Kate knew it, they were back in the castle.

Chapter 6

As Kate was walking down the hall she noticed 5 pictures, of wolves. The first one was a light brown, with a plaque stating "Lord Hagen", the second was a light tan wolf with slight spots of brown, stating "Lord Taylors", the third was a brown with a white spot on its head, stating "Lord Spradin", the fourth was just a plain brown stating "Lord Forestry". But the last wolf was bigger than the rest, black, jet black with black eyes stating "Lord Tipo". My father, the leader Kate thought with a little smile on her face. She returned to her room, finding her father inside. Oh boy what now? Kate thought.

"Nothing my dear, the ball will start at 8:30, so be prepared. But . . . before you come down . . . um . . . dressed, you must present yourself in your lycan form. We will have your dress and belongings downstairs for you, the dress looks wonderful, I'm sure you will be the prize of the ball tonight Kathern." Her father almost had a glow on him, as if he was proud. "Ok dad." Kate sat down on the bed and picked up the book, Marcus came to join her. "Listen Kate, I want you to know that we love you, deeply, and yes I am proud of you. Good luck honey." A tear formed in her eyes as she gave him a hug. Then Marcus stood up and started for the door, when a question popped in Kate's head but before she could ask, he already started to answer. "Yes. Yes I do love your mother, very much." Then like that he was gone. Scamming over the book she found a part about aging. "Once when a lycan reaches 45 human years, they age one day for every year. After 50 human years, they must return to their clan in their destination. A Pure White wolf, however, reaches 25 human years and they quit ageing, they are immortal."

Immortal? No way?! Kate's head started to spin, until she realized she was a pure white, she did have that black spot on her tail, maybe that meant she wasn't immortal, or even a pure white at that. Kate continued reading then realized the time 8:25, she was going to be late. She opened the door to her room and closed her eyes and thought about herself in her lycan from, once when she got the feeling in her stomach, she knew she changed.

As Kate was walking down the stairs everybody stood up and bowed to her. Kate took her place next to her father. With a deep voice Marcus announced "May I have the honor to present my daughter Princess Kathern Tipo. Daughter of Lord Marcus and Allision Tipo." After Marcus's speech everybody clapped their hands and bowed once more to Kate, she bowed her head once and let her mother led the way to the library where Kate retransformed. As Kate was getting dressed, her mother was doing her hair, pulling half of it back with the silver pin. Thank goodness the rumors about werewolves and silver wasn't true otherwise her hair would be on fire Kate thought to herself. The idea made her smile slightly. Once when they were finished Allision led Kate back to the main hall where everybody was waiting for her. Everybody was surrounding Marcus shaking hands and laughing. But despite how many people were there, Kate only noticed one person, Chris. Right at the same moment Kate thought about Chris he glanced over at her and for a moment they made eye contact and exchanged smiles.

Marcus grabbed Kate and started to introduced her to the other clan leaders and their sons but none caught Kate's eye. It was getting close to eleven when Marcus asked if she has chosen anyone. With fear in her eyes Kate stood face to face with him and replied "No, I chose no one here, I want to marry for love, not for this, not like this dad . . ." Marcus's eyes grew pitch black and that sent fear all through Kate's body, she swallowed hard not wanting to her hear father's decision. "How dare you?! Fine, rather you like it or not I will choose for you." Marcus turned around and called for Lord Taylors and his son Leo Taylors.

"Hello your highness," Leo said bowing; taking Kate's hand he kissed it. The thought of him touching he made Kate want to vomit. Marcus bared out his chest and without hesitation said "My daughter has chosen you, Leo Taylors, to be her mate." Kate couldn't believe what was happening right in front of her eyes. Her father, her own flesh and blood just gave her away to a complete stranger. But to Leo the feeling was opposite with delight he asked Kate for a dance, scared of what her father might do if she said no, she agreed.

They enter the middle of the floor. "I'm pleased you have picked me Princess, we both have great strong genes, and our off springs will be great." Leo said as he pressed Kate's body closer to his. As he turned a little bit Kate's gaze met with Chris's again. Looking in her eyes he knew she needed help. He walked up to the couple and polity asked for a dance with Kate. With no hesitation Leo said yes kissed Kate's hand once more and excused himself to talk to Marcus.

"Thank you so much Chris, any second longer and I'm afraid I would have vomited." They both laughed at the joke. "Well that would be a shame, because you look very beautiful tonight Kate." With the compliment Kate blushed and Chris laughed again. But their fun was cut off short when the doors of the castle blew open and in strolled a lycan with red eyes, a rouge no doubt.

Marcus jumped in front of Kate to protect her. "You are not welcome here no longer Victor Veach, leave now or be beheaded." Fangs showing under Marcus's mouth. "Why leave? Already? That's a tad rude don't you think, seeing how I brought a present for your precious . . . princess." An evil grin can upon Victor's face. Out of nowhere he threw a fire ball, heading straight for Kate. Allision quickly threw a water ball to put of the fire but that was just a distraction, Victor already changed and was charging right for Kate. She ran to her left before he could get to her but it was too late, he had driven his claws into her right leg. Kate dropped to the floor, screaming out with pain, blood already soaking the floor. When Kate looked up Victor was charging at her again, but right before he got to her, a giant black wolf cut him off from his path to Kate. It was her father. Marcus threw his fangs into Victor's neck, he leaped out a yelp, but that didn't stop him, he thrashed Marcus around until he finally let lose.

The two wolves circled each other, and then attacked. Victor snapped at Marcus's hind leg, it started to bleed instantly; then Victor bit the side of Marcus's neck, making Marcus yelp out in pain this time. Kate could feel her father's pain. She looked around; everybody was turned except for her mother. Kate noticed a sword near Allision's feet. "Mom, the sword!" Kate yelled out, she could hear her father's voice telling her no, to run but that didn't matter, Kate was not going to let her father die. Victor started to charge towards Kate, she grabbed the sword her mother kicked over to her and right as she turned around the sword went right into Victor's trough. His body went limp over Kate's, his mouth closing down on her hand. Kate yelled and saw the blood that covered her arm, and then everything went black.

When Kate woke up, she had her mother and father standing over her. Marcus's neck only had scratches on it and she couldn't see his leg but she was sure it was only scratches the same way. Finally fully awake Kate started to feel pain in her leg and on her hand. Starting to cry and tremble with pain, her father called for a healer. Minutes later Chris arrived. He unwrapped her leg, held his hands over the deep cuts and his hands started to glow a bright green, then changed to a white color, the pain in her leg was gone. There wasn't anything there, not even a scratch. He unwrapped her hand and held it, the same thing happened, only this time she looked up into his eyes, they were growing, emerald green.

She thought to herself, trying to get a message to him, but using his power has put up a wall, like a blocker. She waited until he was done healing and almost instantly they made a connection. *"You were the one from the house, the messenger right?"* Her gaze never left his, looking down she got an answer *"Yes."* She looked at him again, *"Meet me here in my room at midnight."* All Chris did was smile. He bowed his head to Kate, Marcus, and Allision. "Anything else my lord?" "No that will be all thank you." Marcus rose his hand as a gesture for him to leave. "What you did last night Kathern was very foolish, Victor could of killed you. But you were also very, very brave. I'm proud of you my child." Marcus's words made Kate finally fell wanted, felt loved for once.

"Thanks dad." Kate rolled over in her bed, thinking about Chris, she fell right to sleep. Around 8pm she heard a knock at her door, Kate opened it, and there he was again, Chris, holding her tray of food as usually. "Your dinner Kate." He said smiling. Thinking to their selves, *"You still going to be here at midnight?"* Chris smiled again, "Yes, I will, good night princess." Chris gave her a cute little wink and left.

As Kate was eating, she was trying to recall all the actions that happened last night. First, she is engaged to stranger, second she killed somebody and the worst thing is she has feeling for somebody else, Chris. Finishing eating she picked up a piece of paper and a pencil and started to draw, the tress out her window, the towers, and the fence that blocked it all in. just starting out the window admiring the view she noticed something, it was the owl again, the same one, she was sure of it. It had the same red markings on the tip of its tail. The owl's gaze met with hers, *"Hello Kate."* Kate jumped back surprised, looking around, she saw no one there, no scent or feeling of a lycan. With a worried look on her face, Kate looked back at the owl. *"Yes, I am talking to you."* Kate jumped away from the window. I must be going crazy she thought as she shut the windows. She picked up the book of the blood moon, reading this she learned something new every day, weird things. Things she could never imagine. She returned to the part about guardians, how they can shape shift. Time went by as she was reading, she felt as if everything she knew about her life was lie, and this, this world with lycans and guardians was the real world. Midnight came and then there was a knock on her door, Chris.

Chapter 7

With a smile on her face, she opened the door and there he stood, a handsome young man, lycan, whatever, all she knew was that he was amazing. The biggest smile grew in Chris's face, then Kate remembered. "Sorry, I just . . ." "It's fine." With a smile still on his face Chris asked if he could come in. "Of course!" once when Chris was in the room, Kate shut the door. "So what now?" Kate asked. Chris looked around, realizing there wasn't much to do in the room, so with another handsome smile he asked "You wanna go outside?" Confused Kate didn't understand, they wasn't allowed outside without guards. Chris walked over to the window, opened it and said "Shall we?" still confused Kate walked over to the window looking down, there was no way they could get down there without hurting themselves.

Chris held his hand out the window, his hand glowing bright green along with his eyes. Kate watched as a vine grew from the ground making its way up to window, almost forming like a ladder. Amazed Kate just stood there. "It's perfectly safe Kate, I promise." Chris held out his hand, and without hesitation Kate took it. He led her down the vines very carefully. Once when they reached the ground, they strolled along the garden and found a tree to sit under.

"So Chris Goshen, tell me about yourself. How did you do that? I thought you were only a lycan and a healer. I didn't know you could posse more powers." Kate turned to Chris only to find his head down, as if in shame. Finally he led out a long sigh, "It's quite a long story, I'm sure you would be bored of it." Kate looked around and held up her hands as if what else to we have to do? Chris caught the hint. Eyes glowing he began to talk, "My father is, um, was Victor Veach. When the other clans found out that the Veach clan was going rouge they tried to save the others but it was too late, I was very young then, I don't remember anything but from what the maids and guards have told me. So they brought me here, change my last name and the clan is hoping I can carry on a name, start a new clan, once when my training is finished and I prove myself to the clan leaders." His eyes still glowed green. Kate couldn't believe this, he was royal blood, by choose she could him to be he suitor instead of that despicable Leo. Chris looked at her and smiled. Sending a telepathy message, he said *"That would be nice Kate."* He placed his hand over the ground and a rose bloomed right in front of Kate's eyes. It was so beautiful, so bright and perfect. Chris handed Kate the rose, with a smile she took it, grateful. Eyes still glowing that vibrant green, Kate's eyes glowed light blue like water, they both leaned in for a slight kiss, but something happened, they had a connection like never before, they both felt it.

They sat there for a little longer, holding hands, then realizing what time it was they climbed back up the 'latter' of vines. Chris reached his hand out the window and just as they appeared the vines disappeared. Kate gave Chris one more kiss as she led him to the door. Giving him one more kiss she shut the door. Heart fluttering with delight, smiling she laid down in her bed, she turned to the window, which was still open, she got up to shut it until she realized the owl was there again. She looked the owl in its eyes and said *"Who are you?"* The owl replied *"You know me Kate."* The voice was so familiar, somehow she knew it, it was a young lady's voice. Then the owl flew away. Thinking about Jai, missing her, wishing she could tell her everything, she fell asleep.

The next morning there was a knock on Kate's door as usual. However this time it wasn't Chris, it was Leo. "Your breakfast my Princess." Kate forced a smile, wiped her eyes and said thank you. Leo nodded, sat her tray on the table by her bed and sat down beside her. A strand of blond hair falling down her face, and with a gentle touch he simply pushed it out of her eyes. She could tell he meant her good in all the ways he could. Getting up, he smiled and said "I'll leave you to be, however please join me for a stroll outside later?" Kate forced a smile once more and said "Sure." "Great, good bye Princess Kathern." Leo turned to leave but Kate stopped him with a question, "Is this what you want? I mean being pushed into this . . . this . . . marriage?" Kate could tell she startled Leo with the question. He turned and looked in her eyes and she could tell, feel the sadness. "Kate, I might not be the greatest suitor here for you, however I will promise you this, I promise to take care of you for as long as I can." Then he walked out.

Tears forming in Kate's eyes, the realization came to her. Her father was not going to let her choose Chris, not if he knows he's a Veach. She was going to be married to this guy, but in the meantime she did have two years before she would be wedded, that gave her hope, not much, but just enough to keep her heart from breaking.

Chapter 8

Disregarding Leo's walk, Kate went outside by herself, walking around. She found the tree that she and Chris sat under. With a smile on her face she looked around, then there it was, the same owl. Kate was going to find out what was up with this damned owl. Using telepathy she called the owl to come to her, by order of the Princess. Within moments the owl was there, right in front of her. Kate looked in the owl's eyes fire red. Kate asked *"Who are you?"* The owl looking around, glowed red then transformed, before Kate's eyes, there she was, Jai Manks. Kate jumped back, looked around then took off her coat and wrapped it around Jai.

"What the hell Jai?! Have you been spying on me? Are we even friends?" Kate looked at Jai, her eyes glowing bright blue. Jai looked at her, tears forming in her eyes, streaming down her face. Finally Jai wiped her eyes, and began to speak, "Kate I am a guardian, as you have probably noticed by now, but yes we are friends. I found out what I was when I was 13, then my parents told me about you. I was to watch over you, I was suppose to teach you our ways, the ways of the clans. However you left and I had to fulfill my duties. So I followed you here."

With more tears coming to her eyes, Jai looked at Kate, held her hand and said "Kate I know about you and Leo, but I can feel your feelings for Chris. I was here last night, watching over you two. I'm sorry." Kate sighed and leaned against the tree. "My whole life has been a lie Jai, I have feelings for Chris and I can feel he has the same feelings for me, but my father would never approve, I don't want to marry Leo, I don't know what to do Jai." Jai looked at her best friend in pain, not knowing what to say, she just sat there holding her, trying to comfort her.

"Kate you have to tell somebody, your mother would understand, talk to her." Jai said desperately trying to comfort Kate. Kate looked around, remember the rose, the kiss, she knew that's what she had to do if she wanted to be happy. "Meet me in my room in a few minutes, but as your owl form, you can help me, I've learned to block people out of the telepathy, like a wall." Kate stood up, waiting, Jai glowed red, then fluttered out from the coat. Jai flew and landed on Kate's window seal. With a deep breath Kate went back into the castle, demanded her mother to be summoned in her. Kate opened her bedroom door and there was a rose with a note.

"*Kate, I miss you please meet me outside at midnight tomorrow night. C.*" Kate smiled as she smelt the rose, she smelled Chris's scent. "*You're in love right Kate?*" Jai's voice streamed through Kate's head, with a smile, Kate nodded. There was a knock at Kate's door and walked in her mother. "You asked for me Kate?" Kate looked at Jai and then turned to her mother, "Yes mom, we need to talk, but only us, I do not want dad to find out." Allision nodded and sat down on the bed beside Kate, noticing she was holding a rose. "I see your suitor is taking a liking to you Princess." Allision gave a slight smile to her daughter. Kate nodded and took a deep breath, and came to the courage to say what she wanted.

"That's the thing mom, I don't want to marry Leo, there's somebody else, his . . ." Allision cut her off "Name is Chris, Chris Goshen, the young guard." Kate looked at Jai, surprised. Her heart felt like it was going to explode. "But how did . . . ?" "I'll explain Kate, but first," Allision looked at Jai who let out a 'woo' trying to keep up the appearance. Allision went to Kate's closet and came out with a pair of extra clothes. "Jai, you can come out now." Much to both Kate's and Jai's surprise, Jai flew into the room and retransformed. Handing Jai the clothes, Allision at back down by Kate, still speechless, frozen Kate had no idea what was going on, again. Jai got dressed and sat down on the floor between Kate and Allision.

Allision took a deep breath before she spoke like it was going to be her very last words, which to Allision, she need that it could very well be. "18 years ago, right before your father and I was courted the Tipo castle got a message from a guard reveling that the Veach clan was going rouge, all of them. Since I was still your father's guardian, I went with them to help destroy the clan. When we reached Victor's castle, they were gone, or so we thought. Victor and his wife Rein jumped out and attacked us, still with the hunger for blood. Rein was killed during the fight but afterwards, Victor fled. Obeying orders giving to us from the council, we sat the house of fire. Walking away I heard a cry, a babies cry. Using my water abilities I was able to go back into the castle. I followed the cries until I came to a room where the baby was, in a crib crying, green eyes, I knew right away he wasn't rouge.

We didn't know his mane, so I named him Chris, Chris Goshen. Much to everybody's surprise, his powers developed quicker and stronger, and it was like he devolved at new power almost every year. He is every unique my dear. When we went into town to get your dress for your ball, I knew right away you picked it out because of its colors, green just like Chris's eyes. I knew then what I had to do. So I arranged him to be the one to deliver your meals. I can feel the way you feel about him, and it's amazing. You and Chris have a bond of sometime, something special. I've already talked to Chris, he would be please to be your suitor, and yes, although his name isn't royal, his blood is. You may see him if you wish, however you must keep up this masquerade with Leo until the time is right. Understand?"

Frozen with shock, Kate nodded her head, she couldn't even find any words to say. Allision rose up, "Jai, under my permission and that of Kate's, you are now welcomed to join us for the remaining of our stay. Tomorrow some escorts will take you girls into town. Go have fun, go shopping, laugh and be teenage age girls again. But under no circumstances is any of this to be repeated. Understand girls?" With eyes wide open they both nodded their heads together.

"Good, good night girls. Oh and by the way Kate, I do believe you have a visitor." Allision tilted her head towards the window and Chris was there, sitting in the window seal. Seeing the smile on Kate's face made Allision feel happiness knowing her daughter was happy and was going to get what she wanted at least that is what Allision, hoped, prayed. Kate jumped off the bed and gave Chris a huge hug. They shared a very passionate kiss. Jai cleared her throat meaning she was still there. "Oh, excuse us. Jai this is Chris, Chris this is Jai, my best friend'. Chris and Jai shook hands and for the rest of the night, they stayed up, talking, laughing, being happy, they way it should be. As the night ended, Chris gave Kate another kiss, and left out the window just the way he came in.

"Kate I really do wish you two the best and I pray that it can work out for you too. You guys are so happy together, it's almost like you

Ayla Jimenez

have a glow between you two. You can tell you two are falling in love. I couldn't be any more happier for you Kate. "Thanks Jai." Kate walked over to Jai and gave her a hug. The two girls stayed only a few more minutes before deciding about to bed. That night the only thing Kate thought was Chris, and his eyes. How to Kate he was a vision from heaven.

Chapter 9

With two knocks on her door, Kate woke up quickly, excited, until she saw who it was, Leo. "Good morning my dear, I've brought you your breakfast as usual, oh, I see you have a guest." Kate turned to look at Jai, looking back at Leo, "Yes, This is Jai Manks, she will be staying with us for a while." "Oh, well I must call for another plate of food for our guest." Leo turned around to walk out the door. "Oh Kate I almost forgot, your vehicle is ready whenever you ladies are." Leo kissed her hand and walked away.

Within an hour, the girls were running down the stairs to the door, Chris stood by the door as a guard. "Your highness." Chris said with a smile and then bowed to her. Kate smiled and so did Jai, seeing the connection they had as they walked outside. The sun finally showed some, reviling the trees with snow that almost made them sparkle like they were diamonds. The girls drove into town, parked and started walking around, looking at all the stores. Kate bought a blue sweater and Jai bought a lot of extra clothes, a lot with red in it. Finally the girls stopped a park to eat. "So that Leo guy, that's the suitor your father picked out for you?" With a discussed nod Kate replied "Yes." Jai smiled a little bit, "Well he's not that bad looking Kate." With a smirk little smile Kate said, "Well by all means Jai you can have him." Then an idea popped into Kate's head. Turning to Jai, Kate smiled. Jai looked around and then looked back at Kate. "Um . . . What?" "Jai, you could distract him, make Leo like you, You could be with him, and then sooner or later he would have to tell my father." Jai looked at Kate like she was crazy, but it did make sense and if it was the only way Chris and Kate could be together, Jai would do anything, besides Jai thought he is very cute. "Great so you'll do it? Please?" Kate was partially begging. Jai sighed, lifted her shoulders and said "Why not?" Kate partially tumbled over on top of her giving her a hug, but soon Kate got a sense of something and it must have been close because so did Jai. Kate looked around until she spotted a man in the distance, wearing pitch black, a lycan no doubt, however his eyes were glowing red, then a message entered Kate's mind, "Hello Princess, soon enough, he was gone, vanished. Kate stood straight up, fear in her eyes.

Jai knew they need to go. They walked back to the van, caustically. On their drive back to the castle, Kate was thinking, the stranger's scent, it was just like Victor's but Kate couldn't make anything out of it. When they reached the castle, she asked to guards to summon her father.

Kate was waiting in the downstairs room, pacing, nervous, fear over whelming her. As Marcus entered he already knew what was wrong, her thoughts were very deep. "Dad, do you think there's going to be another attack?" Marcus sat down in a chair, his hand on his head. "I don't know Kathern. But what on earth were you doing in town? Alone at that?!" Kate looked down, "Jai's here dad, we went to town to get her some clothes." Marcus nodded his head and left.

Kate sat there thinking, then Leo walked in. keeping her thoughts clear and trying to block them, she said, "Hello, Mr. Taylors." Leo laughed. "Kate, if we are going to be married then please no more of the Mr. Taylors thing, just call me Leo." Kate nodded and sat down, with Leo joining her. "Something's bothering you my dear. What is it, if you don't mind me asking?" Kate looked at Leo, sighing she asked questions about how he was suppose to 'suit' her. "Well from your father's instructions, I'm just suppose to be here with you, get to know you, and once when we are comfortable with each other, then we start the wedding plans." Remembering what her mother said, Kate knew she had to go along with it. "Very well." She added.

She sensed Jai was close and asked her to come into the room, within minutes, Jai was standing in the door way. "Leo, Jai will be my brides' maid so I think it's best for the two of you to get to know each other. After all she is my guardian." Leo nodded with agreement, as Kate left. Uncomfortable, Jai sat down across from Leo. Her eyes met with his, and he thought about how much her eyes had a fire in them, how beautiful they were. "So you and Kate are already making the arrangements for the wedding?" Jai asked. But much to her own surprise, Leo sank down in his chair, looking at her, he knew he needed somebody to talk to, and here she was. "Well, to be honest, I don't want to marry Kate, not like this. Call me old fashion but I want to marry for love, but when Lord Tipo told me Kate choose me, I was actually a little disappointment." What a conscience, Jai thought. "Well," Jai started, "We must not let Kate know. But don't worry," Jai leaned in and whispered in Leo's ear, "Your secret is safe with me." Somehow he felt a spark, warmth fell over his body. As Jai walked away she could hear his thoughts, *"What am I doing? I can't have feelings for Jai, but those eyes, her words . . ."* Jai felt as he continued in his 'fantasy'. She shut the door and ran up to Kate's room, however Kate wasn't there, but her window was open, Chris Jai thought. Jai glanced out the window and saw them holding hands, running around, laughing. She transformed and flew down to them, her and Kate's eyes met. *"It might turn out easier than what you think Kate. He doesn't want to marry you either, and now I'm pretty sure he's getting a thing for me."* Kate's smile grew wide, this can work she thought. Kate turned to Chris, his eyes big with delight and a smile showing he now knew their secret plan they came up with. Chris looked at Kate, he felt somehow, they were meant to meet, to be together, to fall in love, and that gave him delight beyond words.

Chapter 10

Within a week's time, Jai and Leo was spending every moment talking about the 'wedding' plans. As for Kate and Chris, their bond grew stronger and stronger every day. Chris, Kate, and Jai were walking outside along the castle when a flash of something ran in front of them.

Chris standing guard, Kate transformed and Jai glowing in flames, all three waiting for the attack. Then the figure formed right in front of their eyes, the body forming, like black specks, then he appeared.

"Hello brother." The man, eyes glowing red, looked at Chris. Chris's eyes started glowing bright green. "Cole what are you doing here?" Cole looked right at Kate, "She really is pretty brother, no wonder you fell in love with her. But too bad you don't want to share." Chris's anger over whelmed him and he started to charged towards Cole, but he was too fast for Chris. He slid from side to side, missing each of Chris's blows. Cole ran over to Kate, facing her. She growled, blaring long white fangs. "Oh, such a temper, I love that in a woman." Cole smiled, turned to Chris, Jai's eyes glowed red, she threw a fire ball at Cole. Quickly he turned around and caught it, and flung it towards Jai, she dropped dodging the fire ball, that landing ion a tree, catching it on fire. Cole smiled and vanished. They stood, waiting for another attack, then after a few more minutes they relaxed. Noticing the fire, Kate put up her hand and instantly the fire went out. Turning, looking at Chris, Kate knew he had more to say but before anybody said anything, the castle guards came running out of the castles doors, along with Marcus, Allision, and Leo. Kate and Chris departed, keeping their distance.

"What is going on here? Explain now!" Marcus yelled out. Bowing on his knee, Chris Stated, "My lord, Princess Kathern and Miss Manks were outside for a walk and as a guard I was here watching over them, however we were attacked." Chris held his head down, hoping Marcus believed him. Leo's eyes focused on Jai, but remembering Kate was there, he ran over to her. "My Princess, are you ok?" he asked sounding concerned. "Yes, thank you Leo." Leo bowed his head to her answer. Looking at Jai, realizing she was fine as well gave him an overwhelming power of relief. He bowed his head one last time and left them to be. "Mr. Goshen, may I see you in my quarters, now please." Marcus's question was merely a demand than a question.

With fear rushing through him, Chris got up and followed Marcus. The guards left and Leo followed them. Allision stayed behind, looking at Kate asking if everything was alright. Kate nodded. Her mother bowed her head, "Good night my dear, good night Jai." They both said good night to Allision as she left. Kate and Jai went to her room, trying to relax from what just happened.

Meanwhile in Marcus's quarters, Chris was very nervous. "Please, do not be afraid, Mr. Goshen, Chris, isn't it?" Chris nodded quickly. "Chris I owe you a great deal of respect, for protecting my daughter and Miss Manks." Chris was surprised, stammering he finally said, "Umm . . . umm . . . thank you sir, your sire." Marcus nodded. "Do you know who it was, the attacker?" Chris quickly blocked his thoughts, "No, sir, but I do know it was a rouge." Marcus thought for a moment, "Very well, thank you Chris once again." Chris nodded and stood up heading for the door; Marcus stopped him and spoke again, "Oh Chris as you know, the night after tomorrow is a full moon. You must join us for the hunt." Surprised Chris smiled and with delight said, "Of course sir, thank you." Chris shut the door, the hunt, only the royals go out for the hunt. Maybe he was finally being accepted. Remembering the fight that just happened he knew he must go and explain to Kate. He walked up the stairs to Kate's room and knocked but nobody answered. Thinking she went to bed he started to walk away, until the door opened. Kate was standing in the doorway eyes glowing bright blue, Chris knew she was mad.

"May I come in? Please Kate?" Kate sighed, her eyes returning to their normal blue color, she opened the door. Noticing Jai was there, he opened his mouth to speak but Kate stopped him before he spoke.

"Don't worry, I will go, I need some fresh air anyways." Her eyes glowed red and she transformed and flew out the window,

Kate turned to look at Chris, "Got something to explain?" She asked, crossing her arms. Chris sat down on the edge of the bed and said, "Yes, that rouge, was Cole, Cole Veach, Victor's oldest son, my brother. With the death of my father, he became the leader. Now, sensing us growing stronger and knowing that I care for you, he's came to . . . umm . . . claim you, to take you away from us, from me." Confused Kate asked "Why? Why me? What is so special about me?!"

Kate sat down besides Chris. "Well," Chris started, "You are a pure white lycan, you are the next in line to be queen, and I want you, for myself, which he knew almost instantly. So now he's going to try to take you. I didn't know he knew where I was. I wouldn't mean you any harm Kate, I promise. I'm so sorry." Chris's eyes started to tear up, Kate hugged him, trying to comfort him. She leaned in his ear and without hesitation said "Chris, I love you." Chris looked at her, heart full of happiness, "I love you too Kate." That night was the first night Chris stayed with her in her room; he stayed to be close to her, but even more to protect her.

That morning there was a knock at Kate's door, both Chris and Kate jumped up. Chris hurried and grabbed his shoes and went out the window. Just in time when Leo opened the door, "Oh, Leo, good morning." Leo smiled, and then the smile simply faded away. "Umm . . . Kate I have something I have to confess to you, well, um . . ." Kate sat up, already knowing what he was going to say. "We need a meeting, the four of us."

Chapter 11

Kate, Chris, Leo and Jai all sat in one of the many hidden rooms in the castle that Allision had showed Kate. Kate finally spoke up after a few moments of silence, "Well, here's the time to confess a few things. Leo, I know you and Jai have something going on, but there's something I need to say, I don't want to marry you Leo. I love Chris. So for now on . . ." Leo stood up, "We need to act like we like each other, make everybody believe everything is fine." Kate nodded. "We have to keep this hidden, if anybody finds out, then we all will be in trouble." Everybody agreed, and Kate felt a relief fall over her. All together they thought this will work.

Leo and Chris left the hidden room which happened to be behind one of the many book shelves in the library. Kate and Jai stayed in the room to talk. "I am so glad that we got that out of the way Jai . . . I can't tell you . . ." Kate started to talk but Jai cut her off. "Kate, we have to tell your father, before he finds out the wrong way. We both know that's not going to be pretty for any one of us, and if he knew your mother was in on this . . ." Jai stopped, the thought of punishment from Marcus sent chills down both Kate's and Jai's body. However, Kate knew she was right.

She decided she would tell her father the night after the hunt, she didn't want Chris to lose his only chance to be in the hunt for the first time. The rest of the day went slow, Kate and Leo stayed together to keep up the appearance, however they both knew what was on each other's mind, Chris and Jai. They talked a lot, Leo told Kate how he felt about Jai; however he really didn't know what love was, his family never left the Taylors' castle in Rome. He was raised to learn how to court a lady, learned early what his expectations from his family was. But all that changed when he met Jai, to him none of that mattered. He even told Kate how he wished Jai and he could leave and start living their lives the way they want. Kate told Leo about Minnesota, how she always wanted a little quiet home in the woods, and now how her plans included Chris.

Kate told him how her and Jai grew up together, as best friends, and how nice it would be to have him and Jai living next door to them. They both laughed and smiled at the thought of actually marrying for love, bearing children because they wanted them.

Chris and Jai spent most of their time outside, Jai flying around the castle, keeping watch, as Chris was on the ground, trying to pick up any scents from Cole. The day ended with Leo walking Kate to her room, knowing Jai would be there soon, she offered him to come inside. Leo was pleased with the offer but explained that the night before the hunt all the males kept away from their mates, and slept all day until it was time to change and go for the hunt. Kate gave Leo a hug and told him good night. Leo bowed and said, "Good night, Princess." Kate smiled as she shut the door. She turned around and sure enough Jai was there, lying on the extra bed Kate requested for her.

"How did things go today?" Kate asked. Jai gave a shrug of her shoulders, "Ok, I guess. Chris and I spent most of the time outside. He's afraid Cole will try to show up again and attack. Oh by the way, he asked me to give this to you." Jai handed Kate a letter tied in vines with a little blue flower in the middle. Carefully she plucked off the flower and smelt it, Chris's scent was all she could smell and that made her happy enough. Ripping off the vines, Kate read the letter

"*My Dearest Kate,*

I'm so sorry we couldn't see each other tonight; I'm sorry how I won't be there to watch over you. I must rest for the hunt. Jai and I had a great day talking, I've learned a few new things about you my dear. We searched most of the day looking for Cole, but there was no sign or scent of him. So sleep well my love, for we will be together soon. Love Truly, Chris"

Love Lives Forever

Kate sighed with happiness, and then remember her talk with Leo, Kate told Jai how he felt about her, although Kate knew he was in love with her. The two girls giggled and laughed about talk of love and how happy they were that they found it, in the most unexpected way possible. They always talked about planning weddings and having a family growing up, like normal teenage girls do. After about two hours of talking, the girls said good night to each other and fell asleep, happy.

Chapter 12

Kate woke up early that morning, before anybody served her breakfast. She grabbed a clean pair of clothes and went to the bathroom to take a shower. After drying off and getting dress, she combed her hair and started to braid it, wishing how she could be with Chris, she closed her eyes, and then got the strangest feeling inside her. When she opened her eyes, she was inside the guards sleeping cells, dizzy she focused on who she was standing in front of. To her surprise it was Chris! What the hell she thought. Trying to figure out how she got there. Chris woke up, sensing Kate was near, but it startled him exactly how close she was to him, right in front of his bed. Getting ready to speak Chris held his hand up to his mouth.

Using telepathy they connected. *"What are you doing in here, how did you get in here?"* Chris looked at Kate as she stared back at him, confused. *"I don't know. I was in the bathroom, fixing my hair and the next thing I knew, I'm here. What the hell just happened?"* Chris got out of bed, just in his shorts Kate saw how muscular he looked, how perfect his body was. "Thanks." He said looking at her. Kate suddenly blushed and looked away while he put on a pair of jeans. He grabbed her hand and led her down a long hallway, trying to be as quiet as they could, until they came to a door. He whispered very low but Kate could hear everything perfect. "You shimmered. I can't explain what that is right now but I will. Read the book, I'm sure it has something in it about shimmering." He gave her a slight kiss on the lips then shut the door. He couldn't believe it, she must be a pure white, otherwise she would have never been able to shimmer. He returned to bed, thinking about what just happened, thinking about Kate, he fell right back to sleep.

Kate looked around at where she was, she was back in the library.

How many hidden rooms are there in this damn castle she thought? Remembering the word 'shimmering' she quickly ran up the stairs to her room. Jai was already awake when Kate opened the door. Seeing the stress in her eyes, Jai asked what was wrong. "I, I don't know exactly. Do you know anything about shimmering?" Kate asked. Jai looked puzzled but answered, "Yea, umm . . . I guess only rouges can shimmer, that or a pure . . ." Then Jai caught on. "Kate, did you shimmer?" With wide eyes, Kate nodded, "To Chris. He told me to look it up in the book." Together they quickly grabbed the book and started to flip though the pages, and then they found something, reading out loud together, "A rouge lycan can posse many powers, possibly all of them." Well, Kate thought that doesn't really help, or make me feel any better. Then she remembered what Jai said, a Pure White lycan. Kate quickly turned the pages to a chapter all about the pure white lycan. Looking over the words Kate found something, "The Pure White Lycan has merely been a myth, until one actually appeared. No lycan knew of this kind; however they learned many secrets from the stranger.

The pure white posed every power possibly known to the clans. Then one day, just as he appeared, he disappeared never to be seen again." Kate turned the page, and there he was the first Pure White lycan. It was a drawing of course and on the next page there he was again in human form. Looking at the picture both Kate and Jai gasped. The Pure White looked just like her father, Marcus. Then noticing something even more unbelievable, the pure white had the same scar on his chin, just as Marcus had.

Both girls knew that had to be him, Marcus must be the first, but how? Marcus told Kate the scar was from a working accident before she was born. Full of more questions Kate knew she had to get some answers now. As she got up from the bed, Jai quickly grabbed her arm to stop her, knowing what she was thinking, Jai said "Kate, before we assume anything, let's see if you really are a pure white."

Confused, Kate didn't quite understand. Jai sat Kate back down on the bed. "The book said that the pure white can posse every power possible . . . so try something." "Like what, Jai? What am I suppose to do?" Kate asked, almost alarmed. Thinking, Jai finally said, "Transform. Try to shimmer again, try to use fire power, something Kate. You do not want to wake your father up, before the hunt." Kate was thinking, then she closed he eyes and was thinking about outside, she got a tingling sensation in her stomach and then she felt a breeze. She opened her eyes. There she was, outside. Jai stood in the window watching, in awe. Kate ran to the castle walls thought of the vines, her eyes still glowed bright blue but her hand was glowing green as the vines started to grow up the walls to her window. Kate started to climb up the vines to her room, crawled in the window. Then without using her hands, she thought about the vines, and they started to disappeared. She turned to Jai, with wide eyes; Jai bowed and said "Princess, the pure white."

All day Kate and Jai spent outside, practicing trying all the powers that they could think of. Kate was able to transform into an owl, she used the powers of water, fire, earth, and air. She even learned levitation, and catch the fire balls Jai threw at her, just like Cole was able to. Night fall came quickly, so Kate and Jai returned to the castle to Kate's room.

As they walked inside all the men was preparing for the hunt.

Kate, Jai, and Allision watched from Kate's window as all the men waited for the moon to fully rise, Marcus slowly led the way into the woods and the other men followed, one by one they transformed, colors changing transforming into wolves leading onto the dark woods. After a moment of silence, Kate turned to her mother. "Mom, tell me about the pure white. It's dad isn't it? I read about it in the book, there was a picture, a picture of him. He's the first isn't he?" Allision sighed; she knew this day would come sooner or later, more secrets to be revealed.

"Your father was the pure white, but once when you were born, his powers passed to you, and slowly his color faded away, he turned pitch black. He picks a new wife every one hundred years. Soon he will leave and return in 50 years to claim a new one. Yes, your father was the first, since before the book, in fact he even wrote the book. He left it with one of the clans and slowly it made its way back to him, and that's how it got to you. In all of his very long life, he has never reproduced a pure white; you are the second pure white in the history of the lycans clan. That is why you are so special to him Kate. You will get to live a very long life Kate, the same as him."

Kate held her head down, living forever, knowing that she will get to see the ones she loves past away, their children, and their children's children, watching the world change, it was too much for her, she wanted to disappear. She closed her eyes, blocked her mind from her mother's and Jai's. When she opened her eyes, she was in the hidden room. She stayed there for the rest of the night. She laid down on the couch, curled up in a ball, and cried herself to sleep.

When Kate woke up, she was still in the room. She didn't want to leave, she just wanted to hide out forever, but knowing that somebody will be coming to look for her, she shimmered outside. Looking around, she noticed it was a bright day, and she wanted to be free. She closed her eyes and transformed into an owl and flew into the wood. From Kate's window Jai watched her as Kate flew away, Jai transformed and started to fly towards Kate, following her. They flew by each other until Kate noticed a tall tree; she flew to the top and perched on a branch, able to over look the castle.

To Kate the silence was wonderful, but Jai had some things to say that couldn't wait. *"You know Kate, everything will work out just fine, there might be some things in your way, but you are strong and I know you can get through all the troubles the world would throw at you. Chris has been really worried about you Kate. He won the hunt. They are going to throw a dinner party in his honor for winning. He really wants you there, he needs you there for him Kate, you cannot give up now."* Kate thought about going back to be with Chris, to have him hold her in his arms, but then she realized, she didn't have a choice, she had to 'be' with Leo. Kate decided that tonight was going to be the night, she was going to tell her father.

Chapter 13

Kate and Jai returned to the castle, preparing for the dinner. Jai wore a red dress that looked amazing; she pulled her hair back out of her face with bobby pins. Kate wore a jade green dress and braided her long blond hair, over the past few weeks she never noticed how long it was getting.

Together Kate and Jai strolled down the stairs into the dinner room, where at the deep burgundy table, sat six chairs. Allision sat one end of the table where Marcus sat at the opposite end of the table. Next to Allision sat Chris, dressed in a black tuxedo and a blue tie. Next to Marcus sat Leo, dressed in a blue tuxedo with a black tie. Kate took her place next to Leo, and she happened to be across from Chris. Jai sat next Chris, which happened to be across from Leo.

The six of them sat and at in silence, then after dinner, talked about the hunt, how Chris caught the fox, as Marcus and Leo described it, Chris begun to blushed. However his eyes didn't want to leave Kate's vision. Kate, however, kept to herself as did her mother. When everything was said and done, Marcus asked both Chris and Leo to leave, said he will talk to them later. Both guys got up and bowed to Marcus. Kate's heart dropped, Jai sending her a message said *"It's now or never Kate."* Kate knew she was right. For a moment of silence, Kate contemplated the ways to explain. Finally her courage grew and she spoke.

"Dad, there something I need to talk to you about." Marcus sat up, listening, waiting, trying to read her mind, but she learned to block it, smart girl he thought. "Go on Kate." Marcus nodded once. With a deep breath, Kate continued, "Dad, I know about the pure white, I know it was you and now your powers have been pasted to me. However there is more to say." Kate stood straight up, eyes glowing bright blue, Marcus knew he wasn't going to like this however he allowed her to talk.

"I don't want to be courted by Leo, I've chosen a suitor, I want Chris Goshen to court me." Eyes glowing pitch black Marcus stood up, fast, slamming his hand on the table, making every plate chatter. "Absolutely not! He is of no royal blood! I forbid it!!" then to everybody's surprise Allision stood up, "Yes, Yes he is Marcus and you know it! As long as he is of royal . . ." Marcus threw his hand up; "Leave us Allision, NOW!" the yell of his voice startled everybody. But despite how much Allision was scared she stayed, for Kate, courage for her daughter grew inside her. "No, I will not leave, however if you do not let her be with Chris, then yes, I will leave, for good. I love you, you know that, but I had no choice but to learn how to love you. You might not feel the same way about me, but for your daughter, the pure white, let her choose her own suitor, somebody she actually loves, not somebody she has to learn to love."

Marcus knew she would leave, but one thing she didn't know was that yes, he did love her, unlike anything he's ever felt before. But Marcus was not going to let Kathern choose a member from a rouge clan, a Veach at that, so with a heavy heart, he looked at Kate, "You will marry Leo Taylors. No more questions. Now leave Kate and Jai, now. Let Allision and I talk alone."

Tears grew in Kate's eyes, along with Jai's and Allision, they all knew what the outcome was to be. Kate and Jai left, leaving Marcus and Allision alone. On their way to their room Leo and Chris was waiting but they already knew, they could feel it from the girls. As Kate ran in her room Chris grabbed her arm, but despite how Kate felt, she turned and looked at him, "Chris, this has to end now, please leave me alone." Kate slammed the door in Chris's face. Jai sat outside the door in the hallway with Chris and Leo. Jai explained what Marcus had said, tears forming in Chris's eyes, he didn't know what to do, what to think. Meanwhile, back in the dinner room, Marcus and Allision sat.

"Marcus, you leave me no choose. Tomorrow I am leaving. I hope you live the rest of your life lonely!" Allision stood up and left the room. Marcus stayed in the room, thinking. He just lost Allision, possibly only the only woman he has ever loved, and now he knew Kate would leave him as soon as she could. A single tear dropped from his eye, he never knew he could cry. That night the castle stood quiet, it heartbreak it turned dark.

Marcus woke up in an empty bed, all of Allision's things packed and gone. He got up, got dressed and walked downstairs. Marcus approached one of the guards. "Do you know where my wife is?" The guard stood straight up, "No sire, I do not. She asked for her bags to be placed in a vehicle, and asked the driver to go to the airport. That is all I know." Marcus nodded and thanked the guard. Looking around Marcus noticed one of the guards was missing out of line, Chris, Chris Goshen. He turned to the same guard, and asked where Chris was. "Sir, he said he was going out to run, and hasn't returned yet. Do you need me to send somebody to look for him, sir?" Marcus thought about it for a moment, "Yes, yes I do. And once when he is found I want him sent to my quarters at once." The guard nodded and sent another guard to search for Chris.

Thinking about Kate, Marcus quickly ran up the stairs to her room, and knocked. No answer. He knocked once more and then Jai opened the door, looking in the room, he noticed Kate laying in the bed. "How is she doing Jai?" Jai looked at Marcus, and shut the door, crossed her arms, "Lord Marcus, if I may?" Marcus allowed Jai to continue. "Sir, how would you feel if the one you loved you had to make him leave, and being forced to marry somebody you don't even know let alone like? And the worst part is that her father is the one making her marrying a stranger."

For once Marcus held his head down in shame. Jai looked at him, "That's what I thought My Lord. Last night your daughter cried herself to sleep, as her best friend I promised her I would stay by her side no matter what. And that is what I plan on doing, please excuse me." Jai turned around and shut the door.

As Marcus was walking down the stairs a guard came to him, "My Lord Marcus, I've searched the castle and the grounds outside, and there is no sign or scent of Mr. Goshen." Marcus wondered the castle, with a heavy heart, feeling guilty, feeling incomplete. He asked for Mr. Taylors to be summoned in the library. Marcus went into the library and waited and waited until finally there was a knock on the door. Leo opened the door, "My Lord, you asked to see me?" Marcus stood up, "Yes, Mr. Taylors please come in. sit down." Leo stood straight up, "No disrespect sir but I rather stand." Marcus nodded and sat back down. "Very well, Mr. Taylors. It seems my daughter refuses to marry you. What is your opinion about this?" Leo thought about it, then decided to sit, looking Marcus in his eyes, "My Lord, your daughter is very beautiful and is such a wonderful girl, however, I believe I share the same feelings about the wedding. I would like to marry for love, not being forced into a marriage. You are old, and I know you are very wise, however it seems to me that you know nothing when it comes to the matters of the heart. About love, real love. However it is my duty to carry on the promise I made to both you and my father, I will try my best." All of this was coming as a shock to Marcus. "You may leave Mr. Taylors. Thank you." He dismissed Leo. And sat in the library, alone, and started to cry. He lost his family but no matter what it would cost, he was not going to break the rules of the clans.

Marcus sent a guard to check on Kate, and the answer was always the same, lying in her bed, sometimes crying, always with Jai by her side. His heart grew even heavier.

Part Two

Chapter 1

Two weeks has passed in the Tipo Castle, however, nothing has changed. In fact the castle grew even darker. Marcus tried every day to reach Allision. Kate hasn't said one word to him, she never even left her room. Jai did all of her errands, laundry, grabbing her food for her. For once Marcus felt like he wasn't in control.

As Jai went to town to get some things for Kate, Kate got out of bed and took a shower, crying, she felt broken in pieces. After her shower she returned to her bed, then looking outside, remembering the time her and Chris spent under the trees, she decided to go outside. She closed her eyes, and there she was, under the tree that brought Chris and her together, she sat there leaning against the tree. As tears were falling from her eyes, she felt something hit her hand. When looked down, there was a rose, but realizing she didn't grow it, she looked around, but nothing.

The leaves in the tree above her started to rustle and fall down around her, looking up she saw Chris, jumping down. Standing up, surprised to see Chris, Kate spoke "Chris, what are you doing here?" Kate could see the desperation in his eyes. "I had to come back, I needed to see you. I . . ." Kate cut him off and started to walk away. He ran to catch up with her. "Chris, please just leave, please." Despite what she said Chris continued to follow her. She turned around to face him. "I said to go away, I don't want to see you, I don't want to be around you. Why won't you get it yet? We cannot be together, I'm going to marry Leo and that's that. We are not going to see each other again, I'm done trying to live this fantasy. Good bye Chris." Before Chris could speak, Kate shimmered.

Growing the vines, Chris climbed up to Kate's window only to find the window locked. But Chris wasn't going to give up. He grew a rose on Kate's bed, but she just threw it on the floor. Sending a message to Kate, *"Please Kate let me in, I need to talk to you, face to face."* He didn't receive a message back, but suddenly he heard the windows unlock. He opened them, and there they stood, face to face. He missed her so much, her eyes, her face, he longed to kiss her, and he knew Kate felt the same way.

Finally he spoke, "Listen to me Kate, I found a place far away from here, in the woods. I've built us a cabin. Come with me please, I can't live without you, I won't. Nobody would find us out there Kate, please I'm begging you." Chris got down on one knee as he held Kate's hand, crying Kate watched as he pulled out a ring, in the shape of a rose. "Miss Kathern Tipo, will you please do me the honor of marring me? Because I love you will all my heart. I have since that first day I saw you in the yard." Crying, she shook her head, "Yes, Chris, yes I will!" He picked her up in his arms and kissed her, it was so passionate; it was something they both wanted for a very long time. But Kate cut off the kiss, "Listen Chris, I will meet you under the night of the full moon, while the men are hunting, I will leave and go with you." Chris smiled and agreed to the plan. As he was leaving out the window he stopped and looked back at Kate, his future wife, he smiled. "Oh, there is one more thing." Confused Kate looked at him. "Your mother is at the cabins with me." Even more confused Kate said. "Cabins?" Chris smiled, "Yea, three of them, one for us, one for your mother, and one for Jai and Leo." Kate couldn't believe it. She gave Chris one more kiss, and he was gone. She watched as he went over the castle walls.

Kate was so happy; when Jai arrived she asked one of the guards to summon Leo. Immediately Leo showed up, knocking on the door. Kate quickly opened it and pulled Leo in. when Leo's eyes met with Jai's he smiled. Kate showed them the ring Chris gave her, told them how he had cabins waiting for them, all three of them, how they planned to leave under the full moon during the hunt. Jai and Leo smiled and hugged, both agreed to the plan. And for the first time, Kate saw the two kiss. Then to both Kate's and Jai's surprise, Leo had something to say. "I knew about the plan, I helped him build the cabins. I was waiting for his final return before I did this." Jai and Kate looked at each other, then just as Chris had done, Leo grabbed Jai's hand and pulled out a green diamond ring. "Jai Manks, will you marry me?" Jai smiled and jumped up screaming "Yes, yes, yes Leo I will." Kate couldn't believe this, it was all like a dream come true.

Jai, Leo, and Kate all talked about getting married, but soon Leo had

Love Lives Forever

to leave, so the girls stayed in the room, so happy then Kate remembered, they both were only 16. Grabbing the book, Kate and Jai looked through it, trying to find a loop hole, until Kate found one, reading out loud, "Royals must be wedded on their 18th birthday, however under the full moon, as long as somebody of royal blood was present they may wed whenever." Kate stopped and looked at Jai, and they both smiled. This can work out, this will work out, Kate thought.

There was a knock at Kate's door, quickly Kate put away the book as Jai opened the door. There stood Marcus. He smiled slightly, "I'm glad you finally got out of bed." Still upset, Kate crossed her arms. "Can I help you with something, Lord Marcus?" Marcus sighed, "May I come in Kate?" Hearing the worry in his voice she rolled her eyes and waved her hand, telling him to enter, keeping her ring hidden.

Marcus walked in and sat down next to Kate. "Have you heard anything from your mother? Kate, I'm, I'm starting to get worried about her." Kate couldn't believe what she was hearing, he was worried? What did he have to be worried about? "Your mother." Marcus answered. Kate looked at him. "No Lord Marcus I haven't heard anything from her since you run her off. Anything else I can help you with?" Kate didn't care for him anymore, especially now. He reach over to pull a piece of hair from her face but she jerked away from him. Getting the hint, he walked out of the room, shutting the door behind him. "Kate, maybe, just maybe he is worried about her, maybe he really does love her." Jai looked at her. Kate shook her head, "He does not love her, otherwise he would over never let her leave. He doesn't even know what the word means; it's not his ways Jai." Standing outside of her door, Marcus heard everything, thinking to himself, maybe she's right, I don't even know what love is. Still he walked down the stairs to one of the guards, "Any news about my wife?" the guard shook his head and Marcus, disappointed, returned to the library. There was a note on the desk, he picked it up and read it,

"Dear Marcus,

I'm sorry that it came to this, but I cannot live my life knowing that the man I love does not love me back. Please take care of Kate.

Allision."

Marcus didn't understand, how did the note get here something wasn't right. Back in Kate's room, wanting to learn more about their kind, Kate and Jai read more about the book. According to the book, female lycans are ripe at 18; however a male lycan doesn't fully mature enough to reproduce until the age of 25. Jai looked at Kate and smiled, raising her eye brows. Kate laughed. "Don't even think about it Jai. Besides you can be intimate without actually being intimate. And besides, I want to be married before I do that." Jai rolled her eyes, "Say what you want but don't forget, I can still read your mind sometimes. You want Chris, just admit it." Laughing Kate finally said "Ok, Ok, sometimes I wonder what it would be like, but that's it." Jai smiled a smart smile like "*I knew it.*" As night came, the girls got ready for bed, saying good night, they laid down. Jai was right, something she did wonder what it would be like, her first time. As Kate was falling asleep, all she thought about was Chris.

Feeling something touching her face, Kate woke right up, and then jumped back; she was in bed, with Chris! Looking around she knew she wasn't in the castle, it must be the cabin. "Yes, my love it is." Chris smiled. "Oh, my god, how did I get here?" Still smiling Chris said "You must of shimmered here." Kate looked around. "Oh, well I have to get back before anybody knows I'm gone." Chris grabbed her hand. "There's no rush." Realizing she was only in a tank top and her underwear, she started to blush. "Don't, don't be embarrassed Kate, you are beautiful." He rubbed the side of her face, then pulled her in for a kiss, and then his hands started to rub over her body, like he was studying every curve of her body. Starting to get nervous, Chris looked in Kate's eyes. "Don't worry, I know you want to wait, that's perfectly fine with me, my love." She smiled then she pulled him in for a kiss. After a few moments, they stopped kissing and he held her tight, lying on his chest, Kate never felt more combatable or safe. Drifting off to sleep, Kate rubbed his chest. Chris kissed her forehead, told her how much he loved her, and holding each other they fell asleep.

With the sun shining in the window waking Kate up, she slid out of the bed, gave Chris a slight kiss and shimmered back to her room. Jai was awake, "There you are! Oh my god I was so worried . . ." Looking at her, realizing she was still in her sleeping garments, Jai smiled "Where did you go? You shimmered, to Chris, didn't you?" Eyes wide Jai wanted to know all the details, but reading Kate's mind, she already knew. "You didn't mean to shimmer, did you?" Kate shook her head. "I don't know how I did it Jai, I really don't." Jai looked at her, "Kate your powers are growing, and getting stronger."

Chapter 2

Full of smiles, laughs and giggles, the girls went to town to gather a few extra things for their leave. They looked at dresses, both excited to soon to be with the ones they loved. Kate bought a jade green dress, and Jai got a red dress. They both completed on each other's dresses. Finally leaving town and driving back to the castle, on the back road, Kate got a feeling that they weren't alone, forgetting it, she continued driving until they reached the castles gates. Getting out of the van Kate got that feeling again, but this time, Jai must of felt it too, because she looked around asking, "Who is it Kate?" It wasn't Leo or Chris, she felt a deep power of red. A rouge. Her eyes turning bright blue, Jai knew as well, her eyes glowing red, both girls prepared for the worse.

Cole walked out in front of them, eyes glowing red, fangs showing. "Well, well, well, if it isn't the two brides to be? How's my brother doing Princess Kathern?" He started to circle the girls, Jai glowing red, Kate, scared but waiting for the strike. After coming face to face with Kate, he studied her, "No wonder my little brother fell for you." His eyes still glowing red. Kate looked at him, with desperation she asked, "What do you want?" He looked at her, titled his head, fangs and claws showing he turned to Jai and said, "Revenge, on everybody who killed my family, my father." Then his gaze turned to Kate. "Oh, it was you, wasn't it Princess? You were the one who killed my father!" Then he leaped towards Kate, quickly she simmered behind him, then using the powers of the earth, she held out her hand and vines grew around Cole, wrapping him, bounding him until he couldn't move. Jai threw a fire ball at him, but using water powers he put it, and to both the girls' surprise, he was free. Cole jumped towards

Kate, reaching for her, Kate moved quickly, only to have one of Cole's claws digging into her chin, gashing it deeply. Jai threw another fire ball but Cole disappeared just in time before the fire ball hit him. With blood running down her neck, Kate used healing powers and healed herself, however it didn't go away fully, it looked just like the scar her father had on his chin. The scar still burned, still felt open, fresh. The girls quickly ran into the castle, from all of the commotion and sensing the fear in Jai and Kate, Leo met them at the doors. "Oh my god Kate, what happened?" Realizing she was still covered in blood, Kate sighed.

"Cole returned and attacked us, I have a feeling this will not be the last time he is going to visit. I have to get cleaned up, Jai can explain." Kate ran inside the castle, running up the stairs to her room. After taking a quick shower and shower and changing clothes, she closed her eyes and thought of Chris. When she opened her eyes, she was back in the cabin, with Chris. Her appearance surprised him but he immediately ran to her, rubbing the scar on her chin, he said "Cole." Chris's eyes started glowing green, and Kate could tell he was mad. "Don't worry, Jai and I was able to hold him off, but I know he will return." Chris rubbed his hand through his hair as he sat on the bed, "He's not going to quit Kate, he will continue these attacks until . . ." And then he stopped. Kate went over to him and held his hands in hers. "Don't worry, I'm getting stronger and faster, and my powers are growing. Everything will be fine." Kate tried to comfort him but could tell it was useless; he was still going to worry. Kate kissed his forehead, "I have to get back. I love you." Chris finally smiled, "I love you too. Oh, hey do me a favor and put this in the library without anybody knowing." Chris handed her a folded piece of paper. Kate nodded and she was gone.

Kate shimmered in the library; however her father was there, almost like he was waiting for her. Kate quickly hid the letter in her pocket. "Dad, what are you doing here?" He looked down at the desk, which was when Kate realized he had been reading some books, love books. Confused Kate looked at him, "Is everything ok?" With shame Marcus shook his head, "No, everything is not ok. Everything I know, I've been taught is not to feel love, but when your mother left, something inside me left with her. I don't know what this feeling is Kate. So I've read some books, the way they describe love . . . I think it's how I feel, I think, no,

Love Lives Forever

I know I love your mother. I can't find her; I wish I could tell her how I feel, how..."

"How when you look in her eyes you get a tingling feeling in your stomach. Everything time you touch you wish for more. When you kiss her the world spins and then fir a moment it feels like it stops, just so you can cherish and remember this feeling forever. And when you're not around her, you're not you, you are not complete."

Marcus looked at her, with tear filled eyes; he started to cry, for the first time Kate saw her father cry. "You really do love him, don't you Kate?" Kate's heart dropped, she knew he was talking about Chris, she nodded. "Kathern, I do love your mother, and I know you love Chris, but the ruling has been made, and we cannot break the laws of the clans. I'm sorry." Kate's eyes grew a darker blue, a color her father has never seen before. She stood straight up, and nodded once. "Very well Lord Marcus, I'll leave you to your... um... reading sir." Then just like that she was gone, and Marcus's tears grew even more.

Kate returned to her room, where Leo and Jai were waiting. "I told him what happened outside." Jai said, standing up from her bed. "I've been picking up his scent from all around the castle lately." Leo said, and then he continued. "Chris has been on guard all over the cabins but he hasn't been there yet. I'm going to keep on guard here at the castle." Kate sat down, wondering if Cole was actually going to try to kill her. "Hey Leo, do me a favor please and get this in the library without my father knowing." Kate handing him the paper, "Another one? Ok." Leo took the letter. But something accrued to Kate, what did he mean another one? "What are they Leo?" Kate asked Leo seeming like he knew more than she did at this point. "They are letters, from your mother to Lord Marcus. He can't find her so every now and then she sends a letter to him to let him know she's ok." Kate nodded as Leo left the room. Letters? For what? Was all Kate could think of. Marcus really didn't care, and her mother shouldn't be sending these 'letters' to him, putting ideas of love in his mind, it's driving Marcus crazy.

Chapter 3

𝒦ate focused on her mother, and closed her eyes and appeared in her mother's cabin. Seeing Kate brought tears to Allision's eyes. They ran up to each other and gave each other a very long hug, breaking the hug, Kate asked her mother about the letters. "Well, when Leo comes and visits, he tells me how your father is, and here lately he's been upset, so every now and then, without anybody knowing, I send a letter. I've heard your father thinks he's in love with me; however we both know that's his ways." Kate nodded. "Mom, these letters you are sending dad are making him crazy, you have to stop, and it's only making matters worse at the castle." Allision looked down, "Well, it's a good thing I've sent out my last letter." Kate nodded once more, that was all she needed to know. Changing the subject, Kate showed her mother the ring Chris gave her, they talked about everything they could.

Back at the castle, Leo slipped into the library and left the letter where he usually does. Sitting at the top of the stairs he waited until he saw Marcus walking into the library. Marcus opened the door and sat at the desk, looking down he saw another letter, how was they getting here? He didn't care; at least he knew Allision was fine, until he read this one.

"*Dear Marcus,*

Please stop looking for me, I am not coming back. Soon it will be time for you to find yourself a new wife. I know that you are thinking you are in love with me, but we both know you do not. That is not the way of the Clans. I meant what I said when I loved you, but soon my time will come and I will be gone. This will be my last letter to you, and I have only one request to ask of you, please take care of our daughter. Like you she will have a long life, and eventually she will be queen. But one thing you do not know about her is that she is very strong, like you, but like me, she has a heart, and all you are doing is breaking it for her. I will not stand by your side as you hurt her. So take care Marcus.

Allision."

Marcus couldn't believe this; this was going to be her last letter?
Her surprise letters was the only things that kept him going, kept him sane. For the first time, he grabbed a bottle of liquor, vodka, he thought. Marcus was never much of a drinking but tonight, tonight he felt it was necessary. He sat there, drinking, clenching all the letters Allision has sent him, and then he got a scent, no four of them. Kate, Leo, Jai, and Chris. How was this possible? Looking at the bottle he thought he was already drunk, but he knew what he smelt. One by one, he picked up the letters, each had a different smell to them, but this last one, he smelt all of them. They knew where Allision was, they had to, otherwise how did the letters get here in the first place? Marcus got up, then almost falling, he sat back down. "Guards!" Marcus yelled as hard and loud as he could. Quickly a handful of guards came rushing in. Trying to stand again, then realizing he couldn't, he asked the guards to have Kathern, Miss Manks, and Mr. Taylors down in the library immediately. All the guards nodded at once and left.
Kate, Jai and Leo were in Kate's room when there was a knock at the door. Kate jumped up and opened it, one guard stood there, he bowed and raised back up, "Lord Marcus has requested to see you, all three of you." Then the guard left. Shutting the door, Kate turned and looked at both of them, "This cannot be good. Jai, take of your ring, and try to block your minds please. Something's not right."
Kate, Jai and Leo knocked on the library door, when Kate opened it, she saw her father, sitting at the desk, still holding the bottle of vodka. Marcus tried another attempt to stand, until he felt a rush flowing to his head, falling backwards, he missed the chair and fell. Jai laughed but quickly stopped when Kate turned around and glanced at her. Turning

to her father, Kate asked "Dad, dad are you . . . drunk?" Kate walked over to him, as he tipped the bottle for a final drink, Kate pulled the bottle out of his hand. "Dad what the hell are you doing?" He pulled his arm away from hers, only to fall back again. "Kathern Tipo, do not raise your voice to me, I am your father!" With the surprise jump from her father, Kate jumped back, and held her head down. "Sorry dad. Let me help you up, please? Leo can you please come and help me?" Leo quickly ran over to the other side of Marcus, pulling him up. Kate turned to Jai, "Jai summon one of the maids with a cold wet rag and a bucket, I got a feeling he's going to puke." Jai started to giggle again, "Now! Please Jai?" Kate jumped at her, but Jai did as she was asked.

    Kate and Leo finally pulled Marcus to his feet, half-way dragging him to the couch, trying to lay him down. Jai returned with one of the maids, she handed Kate the rag and bucket, "Princess Tipo." She bowed her head. Kate knew her; she was one of the kitchen maids. "Thank you, Sarah." With surprise the maid looked at Kate, she couldn't believe the Princess knew *her* name, let alone, actually calling her by it. Kate felt the happiness the maid let off. The maid nodded one more time and left.

    Rubbing her father's head, Kate noticed he was holding or more like clutching to a handful of papers. Kate tried to take them from him, but he held on to them even harder. "Please Kate, let me have them." Sensing they were the letters from her mother, Kate allowed him to have them. Kate wiped his forehead, "Dad, are you ok?" she asked, actually out of concern. Marcus looked at Kate, and slightly smiled. "You look just like her, Kate." Confused Kate looked at him, still wiping his head, "What?" "Your, your mother, you look just like her and when you smile, you remind me so much of her when we first met." Leaving from Kate's side Leo went and stood by Jai. "Dad, what are these?" Kate asked about the letters. Remembering why he wanted all of them there, Marcus realized he didn't care anymore. He took Kate's hand and held it. "Kathern, I love you, you are my princess, a real princess yes, but you're my little princess, my daughter. And these," He looked at the letters, "These are from your mother, somehow she's getting them to me. I think, I know in my heart, that I love her. I really do." Rubbing his head, Kate sat there, trying to comfort him, but by just being there, Kate felt like it was enough to him. As he started to drift to sleep, Kate heard him mumble, "I love you Kate, as my daughter, I couldn't be happier." Kate grabbed the blanket and covered him up.

Ayla Jimenez

They left him there, sleeping. Kate gave him a kiss on his forehead and walked away. The three of them walked back up to Kate's room. Leo left them at the door, gave Jai a kiss on her hand and told them good night. Lying in bed, Kate thought about what the letters were for, was her mother trying to get a human side out of Marcus? Trying to make him change his mind? Kate was so confused. Thinking about the letters, Kate fell asleep.

Chapter 4

Taking care of her father, who happened to be drinking almost every night, before Kate knew it, a week's time has passed, only four days left before the hunt, and more importantly, her wedding. Kate was so happy and Jai even cried one night telling Kate how excited she was. Remembering she saw coarsest at 'Formally You' Kate decided her and Jai should go back into town, this time they invited Leo for "protection". Walking around, Leo was more than pleased to buy anything that Jai wanted. When they reached 'Formally You', they looked at more dresses then at the coarsest. Jai found a bright red one that would match her dress. Kate looked at some green ones but didn't want any of them, giving up, Kate was getting ready to walk away until something caught her eye. A beautiful white rose coarsest that sparkled, the strap was mesh with little white diamonds within it. That was the one she wanted, pleased Leo bought that as well for Kate. They also bought some suitcases and some extra clothes. Kate also bought a giant cookbook. Jai and Kate looked over some recipes they might want to try together. Leo laughed at their talk, he told Kate how happy Chris was to marry her. And that made Kate even happier.

When they walked in the castle, Marcus was there. "Mr. Taylors, Jai, leave me and my daughter to talk, now!" Both Jai and Leo jumped when he snapped at them but they followed the orders they were given. "Kathern Tipo, please come with me in the library." Kate immediately knew something wasn't right, so she quickly blocked her mind as she was following her father. "Kathern, I know I haven't been presenting myself in the best way lately. But I have been giving this wedding thing a great deal of thinking, so," He sighed. Kate's heart was throbbing, was he going to let her marry Chris? Marcus continued, "In four nights, under the full moon, after the hunt, you and Leo will be married here." Kate's heart just stopped. This can't be happening, not to her, not now. Kate ran out of the library and ran to her room. Jai and Leo were sitting on Jai's bed, but both could tell the distress in her eyes. "He's going to make us get married after the hunt, here!" Kate blurted out. Jai was speechless and Leo stayed the same way until he stood up to speak.

"Ok, if Marcus is going to make us get married then that night every one of the maids will be here, preparing the marriage. We have to get a different plan to leave." They all stopped talking and thought, then like a chain reaction, they all jumped up and started to talk at the same time. "You could shimmer us out of here." Jai shouted out. It was hard enough for Kate to shimmer herself, let alone three people. But despite her doubts, she allowed herself to try at least one person tonight. Kate held Jai's hand, "Jai I want you to think about the bathroom, I'm going to try to shimmer both of us there." Kate closed her eyes, and thought hard about the bathroom, she got the tingling sensation, but once when she opened her eyes, Jai and her were in the same spot. Suddenly Kate got lightheaded, she sat down until the room stopped spinning, then she stood up, closed her eyes and thought about Chris. She could smell the wood, and she knew she was in the cabin. But she looked around and Chris wasn't there, Kate sat down on the bed and waited.

Time went by but there was still no sign of Chris so Kate decided she would look around the cabin. The cabin had two bedrooms, both with windows overlooking the beds, one was bigger than the other so Kate knew that had to be their room, both rooms had closets. Going downstairs, there was another room, the living room she guessed by seeing a fireplace and one couch already placed in front of the fireplace. From there she found one smaller closet, a kitchen, which was complete with a nice stove and refrigerator. Electricity, nice Kate thought. Continuing to look around she found the bathroom which was a decent size, complete with a toilet, sink, and a nice shower. Walking around Kate reminded herself to make a list of things to get for her future home.

Kate found the main door. When she opened it, the view was breathtaking. She could see mountains in the background, surrounded by trees. Kate always wanted a place like this; it was exactly what she wanted. Hearing a slight pounding noise, she stepped out. To her left there was another cabin, with a light on upstairs, she started to walk towards the cabin until she heard the pounding noise again. Looking to her left, she saw another cabin, with Chris on the top of the roof, where he was placing shingles on the roof. Shirtless, Kate thought he looked wonderful, thinking about surprising Chris, Kate ran back into the cabin and got a glass and opened the fridge, empty. Well, water will have to do she thought to herself. She filled the glass and closed her eyes, she appeared right in front of Chris as he was about to hammer down a nail. Startled, Chris dropped the hammer. "Sorry, but I thought you could use this." She handed him the glass and Chris smiled. "Why, thank you my love." He stood up and gave her a kiss on her cheek, but feeling the tension in her, he sat back down. "What's wrong Kate?" She sat down next to him. "My dad has made the arrangements for Leo and me to be married under the full moon, after the hunt. What are we going to do?"

Chris took a drink, almost drinking all of the water, "We stick to the plan. I will show up for you, I promise." Kate smiled and nodded, he leaned in for a kiss and just as their lips touched, she disappeared. Kate returned to her room where she only found Jai, "Where's Leo?" She asked as she looked around the room. "He left for the night. What are we going to do Kate?" Kate sighed and sat on her bed, looking at Jai she said, "We stick to the plan."

Chapter 5

The next three days went by fast. Kate was able to shimmer all of their packed bags, however, everyday that pasted, Marcus grew happier yet still unsatisfied. Kate and Leo kept up their appearance as they made plans for their 'wedding.' It was all pretend for Kate and Leo, but to Marcus, it was all real. It was his dream come true, not Kate's. But she knew if she wanted her own dream to come true, this was what she had to do, Kate had to keep Marcus going if she was going to be able to be with Chris. Marcus asked for a dinner before Kate's and Leo wedding That night Marcus, Kate, Jai, and Leo sat and ate in silence. Kate didn't want to fight so her and Leo pretended to be the dotting couple in love. Jai sat in silence wishing Marcus could see past their masks and realize the truth behind everything. How each one of them found love in the most unexpected way, how it's a love enough to last a life time, but even longer, and the sad thing is, it's all a hidden love. To Jai, the whole thing played itself out like the plot in Shakespeare's 'Romeo and Juliet', Jai smiled at the thought of the book, she remembered in the 9th grade Kate and her got partnered up in English class and they actually read the book, how they hoped they could find a love like that, without the devastating ending.

After dessert Marcus asked Leo and Jai to leave, told Leo that it was time to rest before the hunt, and before the wedding. Once they left, Kate sat there, waiting for a long speech, how Leo was from a great clan, and can be a great husband. However, there wasn't a speech, not a word, the only thing Marcus did was slid Kate a folded piece of paper, kissed her forehead, and said he was going to sleep. Kate waited until he was gone. Looking down she noticed there was two letters, one from her mom to Marcus, and then one from him to Kate. Kate decided to read her mother's letter first.

> "My dearest Marcus,
>
> I was lying awake in bed last night, realizing our anniversary is two weeks away, it happens to fall on the night of the full moon. Remember the night we first met? It was one of our many acceptance balls. When the guard walked over to me and told me you wished to speak to me, I was so sure you was going to throw me out, because I wasn't from any royal blood, only brought up by the Hagen Clan. When you told me you wished me to your bride, I knew you had to be crazy. Then the year you 'suited' me, you told me how much you'd love my hair down. It was so long and blond, you used to twirl your fingers in it. You knew I didn't want to marry you, but you pushed the issue until I said yes. I felt like I didn't have a choice, the wedding wasn't any where my dream wedding, but out of respect for you, I told you everything was fine, and then I learned to like you. After Kathern came, I learned to love you, but later I realized somewhere, somehow, I fell in love with you. Love happens when you least expect it. Now we are no longer together, after almost 20 years together, I feel lost. I only hope you take care of Kate.
>
> With love always and forever,
Allision."

Kate started to cry, all this time she always thought, always wished, she could find a love that her parents, now she knows, the only love that was there, was that of her mothers. Still crying, she started to read her father's letter.

> "Kate,
>
> I know you will hate me for doing this to you, but eventually you will learn our ways, you will learn to care for Leo, as he will for you. I've lost your mother but I do not want to lose you. Everything I have learned has went against what I know,

from the clans. All you have to do is open your heart Kate;
you never know who will come in.

Love, Dad."

More tears feel from Kate's eyes, he signed dad. Wiping her eyes, she started to walk to her room. When she got there, Jai was already in bed asleep. Grabbing her backpack that she was planning on taking, she pulled out her notebook, placing the letters in it, writing on the top of the page "LOVE-?" Could love exist? Now Kate wasn't even sure.

She simmered to Chris, who was lying in bed, he jumped at the sight of her. "Chris," Kate sighed, and sat on the bed next to him, "Are you sure you want to marry me? I mean do you really love me?" Chris looked at her, head titled to the side, "Kate, there is no doubt in my mind, I love you, I always have, and if I could, I would of have married the moment I kissed you under the tree. Our moment is tomorrow night, I want you by my side, every day, every night, every moment I can have with you is an honor to me. I want you in my life, until the end of the world if I could, I love you Kate," Kate started to cry, Chris wiped the tears from her face, and kissed her. It started out as a soft kiss, slowly backing her on the bed, Chris slid his hand to her back to pick her up, cupping her hands in his face, Kate pulled him in closer. Feeling the passionate in every kiss every touch, Kate longed for more.

Slowing down, Kate kissed him once more, "I have to go, I love you Chris." She closed her eyes and she was gone. Rolling on his back onto the bed, Chris smiled as he looked outside, seeing the stars, he saw a falling star. *A wish, what do I need a wish for? I will have everything I need tomorrow night.*

Returning to her room, Kate laid down, hoping, praying, and wishing everything will go just as they planned tomorrow night. Getting a sudden feeling like she wasn't alone, Kate went to her window. She looked out the window and looked around, until she saw something. Two glowing bright red eyes, down by the tree her and Chris sat at. Cole she thought with no doubt in her mind. Closing the window and making sure it was locked, she laid back down. Thinking about tomorrow night Kate tossed and turned until she finally fell asleep.

Chapter 6

Kate woke up that morning, with Jai still in bed, she grabbed a clean pair of jeans and a t-shirt and took a shower. As usual, Kate combed and braided her hair, never realizing how long it was getting, it now reached all the way down her back. Hearing her own stomach growling, Kate went downstairs to get something to eat. All the maids were too busy preparing for the wedding so there was no food prepared. Kate made herself some eggs with toast and apple juice. After eating Kate grabbed the remaining food and took it up to Jai.

When Kate walked in the room Jai was already up. "Kate, you didn't have to do that, I could made my own food." Jai was surprised to see Kate carrying food somebody. Kate smiled, "It's fine Jai. I went down stairs to make me some and figured you might like some as well, besides what are friends for?" Jai took the tray with a cheerful smile. "Thanks." After Jai was finished eating, the girls went down stairs to the library. Kate grabbed a few books she thought she would be interested in. After looking over some books, Jai sat down at the desk. Looking down at the pile of books, Jai noticed one in particular. William Shakespeare's 'Romeo and Juliet.' Remembering what she thought just the night before. "Kate, what if Chris doesn't show up tonight? I don't even know where the cabins are." Kate realized she didn't even know where the cabins were, she could only shimmer to them, but remembering the mountains she guessed they couldn't be that far away, even if Chris and Leo could get there on foot. "Don't worry Jai, he will come for us, he promised me." Kate comforted Jai with her words sounding confident. They returned to their room with their final bags packed, one each, everything else was at the cabins already. Looking over the book one more time, Kate remembered something that her father said; he said her powers would come from her feelings, her emotions.

"Jai, come here please." Kate held out her hand. "Remember the hidden room? Well I want you to think about that room, also at the same time I want you to think about Leo, the way he makes you feel. How much you care about her." Jai nodded, she didn't need to ask any questions, she already knew what Kate was going to try. Holding hands the girls closed their eyes. Kate started to get the tingling sensation in her stomach, Jai was getting it was well, Kate could feel it. When they opened their eyes, they were there, in the hidden room. Jai grabbed Kate and hugged her. "You did it Kate, you shimmered . . ." Jai stopped; Kate fell on her knees, gasping. Kate felt as if she couldn't breathe, then she got lightheaded, and everything went black.

Faintly all Kate heard was, "Kate, Kate wake up." When Kate opened her eyes Jai was there standing over her. Trying to sit up, she still felt weak. "What happened?" Jai helped her up to her feet and sat her down on the couch in the room. "Kate, you did it. You shimmered both of us here, but then you fainted. Are you ok?" Finally able to stand, Kate looked at Jai. "Yeah, let's get back to the room." The girls opened the door and were back in the library. With Jai's help Kate was able to make it up the stairs to their room.

Going into the bathroom, Kate washed her face in the sink. When she looked in the mirror, she saw herself, still a little bit pale, she looked fine. Kate went back into the room with Jai. The girls stayed up talking about the wedding, the cabins, how excited they were. Before they knew it night fall came and they heard noises from downstairs. Opened her door, both Kate and Jai stuck their heads out of the door. All the men were waiting in the living room, then Marcus came out, dressed all in black. Jai spotted Leo, who was standing next to Marcus.

Raising his hands, Marcus started, "Gentlemen, tonight is a full moon, as always we will join together in the hunt. However, afterwards please join us for the wedding of my daughter Princess Kathern Tipo and Mr. Leo Taylors." All the men started to clap and cheer to Marcus's speech. Marcus and Leo shook hands. "Now gentlemen, let's hunt!" Marcus started to lead the way until Leo stopped him, whispered something in his ear. Marcus and Leo shook hands again and Marcus led the rest of the men out of the castle, however, Leo stayed back. The girls waited and then they ran to the window, they saw all the men transform, all different colors glowing, and one by one they ran into the woods.

Leo came and knocked on the door then opened it without hesitation. Jai ran to him and he picked her up in his arms. "Chris will be here any minute. You girls ready?" Both Kate and Jai said yes at the same time. Kate looked out the window, and waited, then she saw two glowing eyes, and she knew that was Chris, she knew he would come back for her. "He's here. What do we do now?" Kate turned and looked at Leo. "We go."

Kate put her hand out the window and the vines started to grow, just like Chris showed her. Kate, Leo and Jai climbed down the vines and met with Chris. Chris looked at Kate, she was so happy, excited. "Kate, I want you to shimmer to the cabins. Jai and Leo are going to transform and we will meet you there very soon." Kate nodded, knowing that both Jai and Leo got the message, she took Jai's bag and they both transformed. Kate closed her eyes, before she knew it she was in the cabins, she has never shimmered that fast. Running down the stairs, Allision was waiting for her. Kate ran up to her, wrapping her arms around her, "Mom, I'm so happy to see you." "Me too, sweetie, hey don't you have a wedding to get ready for?" Allision smiled when Kate looked at her, smiling.

As Kate started to walk up the stairs, the door opened. Kate turned around to see Chris. She ran up to him. "I was so worried. I thought . . ." Chris stopped her, "I promised you I would come back for you, didn't I?" Kate smiled and a tear fell down her cheek. "Go get dressed. Jai and Leo are getting ready now." Without hesitation Kate ran up the stairs to her room. Allision stood there looking at Chris, "Thank you, I know she loves you, and you love her just as much, take care of her please?" Chris walked up to Allision. "Mrs. Tipo you know I will." She smiled; yes she did know that, he's already proved it. "Please, call me Allision. I'm going to help Kate." Chris bowed.

Jai and Leo was ready and standing outside. Jai's dress was fire red, with a slight slit up the side, complete with a red corset. Leo wore a jet black suit, with a white shirt and red tie. Chris stood there, dressed in a black suit with a black shirt and a white tie. Chris was nervous, waiting, then when the cabin door opened, Chris's heart fluttered. Kate had a jade green dress, with a beautiful white rose corset. And her hair, how wonderful Chris thought, with her hair curled and part of it pulled back with a white clippie. Kate was like nothing he has ever seen before, truly a dream come true. Allision walked Kate over to Chris, taking Kate's arm in his, as Leo and Jai did the same. Allision started speaking. "By under the full . . ." Then she stopped hearing a howling, Marcus ran up to her. "What is going on here?!" his eyes glowing pitch black. Leo and Chris stepped up, Chris spoke. "Lord Tipo, I have proposed to Kathern and she accepted. My Lord, we wish to be married, tonight." Rage grew in Marcus, starting to yell, "Absolutely not! I am forbidding these 'weddings'. And you, Chris and Leo, will be banished from the clans!"

Right as Allision and Kate was about to speak up, an uninvited guest showed up, appearing from the darkness from the trees, eyes glowing red, Cole. Chris stepped in front of Kate, Knowing exactly what Cole's plans were. "Now brother, where did my invitation go?" Chris's eyes glowed bright green. "Cole, leave now." Cole walked up to Chris, they stood there face to face, Kate could see how they were brothers. Cole stopped and looked over Chris's shoulder at Kate. "No, not until I get what I came for. Her." "You touch her Cole, and I will kill you." Chris got closer to him. Marcus finally spoke, "Cole Veach, leave now or there will be consciences." Cole just smiled, clapping his hands together, "Oh, no sir, because you see, Princess Kate and I have some unfinished business to tend to. Killing my father was the biggest mistake your little Princess ever made."

Chris ran into Cole, throwing him against a tree, leaves falling down from the impact. Leo and Marcus transformed and stood behind Chris. Cole swung around and hit Chris in the head with a rock, blood starting to run down his face. "Chris!" Kate yelled out, but that only made matters worse. Quickly Cole jumped over Leo and Marcus and became face to face with Kate. Marcus started running towards Cole, fangs showing, growling. But Cole was too quick; he threw a fireball at him, catching Marcus off guard, falling back. Cole's attention returned to Kate, and then before she could react, Cole grabbed her by her throat, squeezing harder and harder. Kate couldn't breathe, she tried to shimmer but she couldn't focus, right before passing out she saw Chris waking up and transforming, jumping on Cole's back, making him release Kate, her body falling limp to the ground. Marcus ran up to Chris to help him, with Leo there, but it was too late, Chris's jaw saw locked on Cole's throat, blood going everywhere. Cole tried to fight back and then there was a snapping noise and Cole's body fell. Retransforming, Chris ran over to Kate, lying on the ground. Allision kneeling besides her, crying. "Chris, she's, she's not breathing." Chris fell to the ground, he held Kate in his arms, glowing green Chris tried to heal her, but Kate's body didn't move. Crying, Chris held Kate closer to him, glowing more trying to heal her again, until he felt something touched his shoulder. Marcus stood there, with Jai, Allision, and Leo kneeling down besides Kate, all touching Chris. He glowed even brighter, Kate's body started to glow blue, then it stopped. They all sat there, Chris holding Kate's body, crying, "No, no, why her? Why not me?"

Still holding Kate, Chris felt a hand placing on his head, the same side that Cole hit. Looking at the hand, he saw the white rose corset. He looked down at Kate, her eyes glowing blue. "He hit your head, I had to heal you." Gasping, Chris started to cry even more as he held her. "Kate, I thought I lost you." Kate placed her hand on his face, "You will never lose me." Chris smiled and leaned down to kiss her.

Chapter 7

"Mr. Goshen please follow me, same as for you Mr. Taylors." Marcus moved his hand as a gesture for the men to follow him. Chris helped Kate up to her feet, where she stood and waited by her mother and Jai. Chris and Leo followed Marcus into the woods, away from the three women. They sat down near a tall tree, as Marcus began to talk. "Chris, as you already know, Kathern was to be wedded with Leo tonight." Chris nodded and held down his head, now he was going to lose Kate, who was everything to him. Leo Kept his head up as Marcus continued. "However, Mr. Goshen, after seeing what I've witnessed, Kate is clearly very important to you and for you to do what you just did, you allowed me to keep what is important to me as well," Chris looked up at Marcus, they met eye to eye. "So it is my honor to give Kathern away to you, tonight if you wish." Shocked, Chris only shook his head. As Marcus stood up, Leo and Chris followed his every move. Holding his hand out to Chris, they shook hands but Chris pulled Marcus in and gave him a hug, "Thank you sir, thank you so much." Marcus waited but hugged him back. "Please, call me Mark." Chris smiled. Turning to Leo, Marcus shook his hand as well, "As for you, Leo, I will perform the marriage ceremony for you and Jai, if that's what you wish." Leo looked at him, eyes gleaming, "Yes, sir, very much." Marcus nodded his head, "Very well gentlemen, I do believe we have plans, don't we?" To Chris and Leo's surprise he placed his arms around the twos shoulder and they started to walk back.

Allision was holding Kate as Jai was walking in front of them, pacing.

"Jai, will you please quit pacing, you're making me more nervous." Kate looked up at Jai, as she stopped and sat down next to them. "He's going to banish them, Kate, I know it." If her father was the Lord he has made himself out to be, then Kate knew Jai was right. Sitting there made Kate feel like she was going to be sick, then she saw her father come out of the trees and she felt even sicker, until she noticed Leo and Chris behind him. Marcus walked up to Kate, rubbing her chin where the scar was. He looked her in her eyes, "You remind me so much of myself, Kathern. I want you to know I love you and I want the best for you. That's why, I am giving you away to Chris, tonight." Looking at him, Kate didn't know what to say. "Well, let's get you married, shall we?" Marcus looked at her, seeing how beautiful she was, a tear fell from his eye. Kate jumped up and gave him a hung that Marcus thought would never end, but he didn't want it to.

Smiling, holding he hand, Marcus said, "Let's go Kate." Standing as they were before Kate and Chris held hands as Jai and Leo did the same, both couples smiling. With the moon right above them, there was no need for lights. Marcus started "By under the full moon and with my power, I now pronounce you, Kathern Tipo, and you Chris Goshen, Mr. and Mrs. Chris Goshen." Marcus turned to Jai and Leo. "As for you, Jai Manks and Leo Taylors, I now pronounce you Mr. and Mrs. Leo Taylors. You both may kiss the bride." Chris held his hand out as he and Kate were kissing. Hands glowing green, vines started to grow out of the ground, growing up around them, encasing them in it. Flowers blooming out all around, leaving the top open with the moon shining in. "I love you Kate." Kate looked at him, "And I love you, Chris, my husband."

Allison stood back, this was twice now she watched magic happen tonight. Marcus started to walk towards her. Wanting to walk away, something inside Allision told her stay there, as Marcus continued to walk up to her. He held out his hand, hesitant, Allision took it. "Allision, I believe we need to talk, um . . . actually I would really like to talk to you." Marcus led her to her cabin and sat on the porch. After a few minutes of silence, Allision cleared her thought to talk. "Marcus, what you did, allowing Kate and Chris to be together, that was amazing. She really does love him, and he adores her like no other, they share a bond like you couldn't imagine. But how it took you this long to see it I don't know. But you did a great think tonight. Thank you." Marcus looked down, "Yes, but I have lost something just as dear to me, my wife.

Allision, there's something I need to tell you, I love you, I am in love with you. I've been so selfish trying to be this 'Lord' everybody wants me to be, but I want to be is with you. I love you so much Allision." Marcus leaned in for a kiss and right as their lips touched, Allision placed her hands on his face and pulled him in closer, they sat there kissing under the full moon. That night dreams came true for everybody.

Chapter 8

The next morning Kate and Jai made a beautiful breakfast for their first time cooking. After breakfast Marcus returned to the Tipo Castle. Marcus felt remarkable good about himself for the first time since he could remember. However as soon as he walked in the castle he could tell something was wrong. Ignoring the tension he walked into the library with his head held high until a messenger walked up to hm. "Sir, I have a letter for you, sent by the request of the Council." Marcus suddenly felt a lump growing in his though as he took the letter. The young man bowed as Marcus walked in the library. How could the council send a letter to him, on behalf of how he was head of the council for being the oldest. Sitting at the desk, Marcus slowly opened the letter.

> "On behalf of the council, 11 to 12 votes, Lord Marcus Tipo, Chris Goshen and Leo Taylors is request to appear for proper judgment for breaking the laws against the Clans.
>
> Council."

Marcus was being summoned for a judgment, with no doubt about the marriages. Only assuming of previous hearings that Marcus himself had to judge against, he knew that Leo and Chris are to leave the clans to banishment, along with their marriages to be annulled at once. As for his own running, Marcus didn't want to think about his own ruling of judgment. Despite the fear for himself and his family's, he also worried about Chris and Leo's fate. However he knew the worse would come to them all if they didn't show up.

After reading over the laws for the clans, Marcus found a few possibilities, but only one stuck to him. After waiting a few hours, Marcus decided to return to the cabins, which wasn't that far from the castle, only a 30 minute drive. Marcus pulled into the road but since there was no drive ways, he had to walk to the cabins. As he approached out the woods, Marcus was Leo and Chris outside building what looked like a picnic table, he picked up some extra boards and started to walk towards the young men.

Kate, Jai, and Allision walked out of Kate's and Chris's cabin with sandwiches and a pitcher of tea. Marcus smiled at the thought that the girls haven't been married for less than 24 hours and they were already fulfilling their wife duties. Marcus sat the boards next to Chris who was pounding away at some boards, walking up to Allision; Marcus gave her a slight kiss on her check. Marcus tried to think of ways to bring up the ruling without the women knowing and being worried. Noticing how the cabins were not painted, Marcus figured out what to do. Waiting until the women went into the cabin, Marcus started to help Chris and Leo. "Hey Chris, Leo I was planning on going to town, is there anything you guys might need? Or would you like to join me? Take a break. What do you say?" Both Chris and Leo agreed to go.

After telling the women bye, Marcus, Leo and Chris started towards the van, and headed to town. The men went into the hardware store, where Chris and Leo bought extra board and nails. Walking around Marcus remembered how the cabins were plain and thought how the guys could surprise the women by painting them. Chris and Leo thought that was a great idea.

Chris got a light and dark blue colored paint, Leo decided to get light green and white, and Marcus got a salmon color for Allison. The ride back wasn't as talkative as the ride into town. Marcus was still contemplating the options that's they were now limited to, and the fact that he had to tell Chris and Leo. The two of them were talking about what else to make, as Marcus didn't say one word, trying to rephrase how to bring up the topic, until his train of thought was caught off, realizing his name was being called. "Mark? Marcus? Is everything alright?" Coming back to reality, Marcus turned to Chris who was sitting in the passenger seat. "Uh, what Chris? I'm sorry I was paying attention." Chris looked at him, slightly confused, then shook it off as if it wasn't anything. "Well I would like to thank you for everything today, and as I was saying, would you like to join us for dinner? I believe Kate and Jai are going to try their luck at almost everything in their cookbook, but they were going to try pot roast tonight." Laughing at the thought of Kate trying to cook put Marcus in a slightly better mood.

"Sure I would love too." Chris smiled back. "Great, Kate said you like pot roast." Marcus smiled and nodded as he pulled into the drive way. Chris and Leo started to get out of the van until Marcus stopped them. "Chris, Leo there is something we need to talk about." Chris and Leo stopped and looked at each other, shutting the doors, they turned to Marcus. Swallowing hard, Marcus felt the lump grow in this though again. "The girls are not to know about this. We, um, we are all being called for a judgment, for the marriages. Tomorrow night we are to be at the council meeting, what they are going to do, to all of us, is as good of a guess to all of us. However, I think I found a loophole, so I will need you guys to pay attention." As Marcus described the plan Chris and Leo sat, listening to every word he said understanding the plot and what to do. All three of them got out of the van, gabbed their bags and started towards the cabins. That night, Marcus realized he had much more to lose than just Kate and Allision, to him, Chris, Jai, and Leo were family now. He had a family to look forward to seeing, everyday, and he planned on keeping it that way.

The night went by fast, but the next day seemed to drag on. Chris and Leo finished the picnic table, as Marcus started to paint the cabins. As the day went by, night came, faster than what Marcus would thought. After dinner, Marcus said he needed to go back into town for a few more things and asked Leo and Chris if they would like to join them. Leo and Chris respectfully accepted and gave the girls a hug and kiss. When the three of them got in the van, Marcus reminded them of the plan. The drive seemed to get longer and longer until they came to the train station right outside of town. Marcus pulled into the driveway and parked.

They walked into the station, went all the way down the hall, passing innocent by-standers. They came to big wooden door that looked as if it hasn't been touched in years, Marcus pulled a single gold key out his pocket and unlocked the door. As he opened the door, the hinges creaked, sending chills down Chris's body. Looking through the door there was stairs that went beyond the light could reach. Slowly one by one they went down the stairs, shutting the door behind them. With Marcus leading the way down the stairs, candles appeared one by one on the walls, until they came to another door, this time there was no use for the key, as the door seemed to open by itself. Continuing to follow Marcus, they entered a room lighted with what looked like a thousand candles. At the room was a long table, counting there was 11 men sitting in the chairs, with one chair opened. Marcus walked right to the front, stopping just so far enough so everyman could see him, Chris and Leo, stood on both sides of him, arms behind them. One man stood, wearing nothing but pitch black, as well as every other man in there, including Marcus. "Lord Marcus Tipo, we the council, has called you here, along with Mr. Chris Goshen and Mr. Leo Taylors on behalf of two marriages that took place without our permission. The marriages of Mr. Taylors and Mr. Goshen are no annulled by my word. As for you Lord Tipo, your conscience is that you give up your place on the seat of t he council and is here now committed to be held until further notice."

Marcus stood still as the man spoke, but once done, Marcus began. "Council, what I did was to protect the clans. With the proper looking and the care of a doctor, Jai Taylors, Mr. Taylors' wife is pregnant, therefore he could not have married my daughter, for the simple fact that no member of the clans has been casted out as a bastard child. I will not allow it to start now. As for Chris, further inspection has proved him to be the son of Victor Veach, that of royal blood. My daughter has chosen him, and of him being that of royal blood, she has the right to choose him, according to our laws. I will give up my seat as head member of this council if and only if you allow the marriages' to continue. They were preformed under the full moon, with me present. What say you?"

Little mummers began to start around the table, each man turning to another one whispering until a silence fell over the room. The man who spoke before seemed to be tensed after Marcus's speech. He looked even more tensed now. "One by one, member of the council, what say you?" As he said, one by one they stood up and gave their votes. "Charged." "Uncharged." "Uncharged." "Uncharged." "Uncharged." "Uncharged." "Uncharged" "Uncharged." "Uncharged." "Uncharged." The last to stand, Sir Taylors, Leo's Father, eyes fixed on Leo. "Uncharged." That was it, they needed 6 out of 11 votes to get out of here alive with Marcus and that's how it would end. Bowing Marcus said, "Very well. Thank you. As for my seat on the council, I respectfully resign. Council members" He bowed once more and they all started out the door they way they came in. walking up the stairs, Marcus locked the big wooden door.

All three of them were quiet until they got into the van. The first one to speak was Chris. "Marcus can you pull into this store here please?" Without hesitation Marcus pulled in. All three men got out and it seemed they all had the same idea, three dozen of roses for three wonderful, beautiful women.

Chapter 9

The days faded into weeks and the weeks faded into months and soon Chris, Kate, Jai, and Leo were celebrating their 3 month anniversary. That night Chris surprised Kate with flowers, different flowers but their colors blended so well together, Kate couldn't believe how beautiful they were. Chris took Kate's hand and led her to their room, covering her eyes. When he removed his hands, there was rose petals surrounding the bed, with a big white teddy bear with a ribbon around its neck, with the words, "I love you" printed on the belly. Chris knew that Kate wanted to wait till the right moment so he wasn't planning on pushing the issue. "Chris this is so sweet, thank you." When Kate turned around Chris was facing her, slowly heading her to the bed. When her legs reached the back of the bed, Kate jumped slightly, until Chris held her in his arms, he leaned into her ear, pushing her blond hair away. "Don't worry, Kate I got you, and I'm never going to let you go."

The voice, his voice, something inside her told her it would be ok.

Kate knew this day would come but she was still frightened, scared, yet for so long she yearned for his body, and he for hers, she could feel it. Slowly he kissed her neck, moving his hands slowly to her back, pulling her in closer to him, bodies touching slightly. He leaned in for a kiss, lips barely touching until Kate couldn't stand it anymore. She grabbed his light brown hair and pulled him in closer, until their lips met, never leaving. Chris ran his hands up and down her body, knowing every curve of her body. Kate took off his shirt, throwing it on the floor. Chris lifted her shirt over her head, reveling a pink lace bra, with her breast almost bursting out. Chris started to kiss her neck, slowly leading his leading his tongue down past her breast in the middle, until he worked his way down to her jeans, then he stopped. Her heart was racing, she didn't want his to stop and he felt it. He unbuttoned her jeans, slowly pulling them off, reveling a matching pair of pink lace underwear. He kissed his way back up, kissing her neck, as he was kissing her; he felt her hands on his chest, rubbing, until they made their way to his jeans.

She unbuttoned his jeans and started to pull them of slowly. He kissed her, passionately, slowly, they removed their undergarments. That night their bodies mending into one. As the night faded away, morning came, Kate sleeping on Chris's chest as his arm was wrapped around her. Kate slowly and quietly got out of bed grabbed some clean clothes and went to the kitchen to make breakfast. As she was setting the table, Chris came walking down the stairs, wearing a pair of jeans and an unbuttoned shirt, right there Kate wanted him, the same way as last night.

Realizing the smile on his face, she assumed he read her mind, Kate quickly turned away. "Your breakfast, my husband." She said feeling humiliated, Chris walked up behind her, hugging her, embracing her. "There is no shame, Kate. So please do not be embarrassed." He kissed her check. They sat down at the table and started to eat. At first there was an awkward silence before Chris began to talking and before too long, they both were laughing. Chris helped clean up after breakfast, as they were doing dishes; Chris splashed a little water on Kate. Surprised, Kate turned to the sink and sprayed him, as he ran to her the sink sprayer fell and they both were covered with water, sliding around the kitchen, until they slipped. Chris caught Kate and she landed on top of him, her wet hair falling in her eyes, he pushed it away. "I love you Kate Goshen." Kate smiled and replied, "I love you too Chris Goshen." A few moments went by until they decided to get up and start cleaning the mess they made, still laughing.

Then there was a knock on their door, Chris dropped the mop and went to open it, Leo and Jai were standing there, Chris offered them to come in. "You know Chris, the cabins were built to keep the rain out, not in." Leo laughed at the way Chris and Kate looked. Jai walked over to Kate. "Hey, umm... Kate, I haven't been feeling too good lately and I was hoping you would go to town with me. I rather not go to the doctors alone. I think I'm just getting a cold." Immediately Kate shook her head. "Yea, of course I'll go with you, just let me get dressed." Jai nodded as Kate ran upstairs. Jai walked over to Leo. "She said she would go with me, so you can stay here with Chris. We will be back as soon as we can. I love you." Leo leaned in as Jai gave his a kiss on the cheek. Kate and Jai left and started towards the van. "Hey Kate, remember how the book said male lycans couldn't reproduce until they reach the age of 25?" Kate nodded. "Well, I'm not sure, but Kate, I think I might be pregnant." Shock flew over Kate; she didn't even know Jai and Leo were having sex. But all she thought about was what the book said. Maybe Jai was really just getting a cold, the flu, something.

They arrived in town and checked Jai into the doctors, it was slow so they got her in quick. She asked if Kate could come in the back with her, and the doctor respectfully said yes. So all three of them was led into an examining room. The doctor asked Jai all kinds of questions. Then he took a blood sample and asked if Jai could provide a urine sample. The doctor left with both samples, soon an hour pasted.

The doctor finally returned with a nurse and an ultrasound machine. Rubbing the gel on Jai's stomach, there it appeared. What looked like a little peanut with stubs that Kate guessed were the arms and legs, along with a strong steady heartbeat. "Well, Mrs. Taylors, it looks like you have a bun in the oven, congratulations, going on almost three months now. I would like to see you once a month from now on. And I would like you to start these as soon as possible, they are prenatal vitamins." Jai got her prescription and they left, neither one speaking a word. When Kate pulled into the driveway, she finally spoke. "So, when are you going to tell Leo?" Jai thought about it, "Tonight, at dinner." Kate nodded her head. "Well are you excited?" Jai with happiness shock her head, "Yea, Kate I am. I mean I'm going to be a mommy; I'm going to have a baby. You're going to be an aunt. You're not happy Kate?" Kate shook her head, "Of course I am, I'm very happy for you Jai. Congratulations." They hugged and started to walk towards the cabins.

Chris and Leo were sitting on the couch, right where they were when Kate and Jai left. Leo stood up as soon as he saw Jai, "So what did the doctors say?" Jai shrugged her shoulders, "Just a cold, that's all, nothing to be worried about. Who's hungry? How about a nice picnic outside?" Everybody agreed and all helped out making lunch.

After the picnic Chris and Kate treated themselves to a nice bubble bath, it was the first one since they been married. Chris massaged Kate's back, kissing her neck. "So everything's ok with Jai?" "Yea just a cold, it will past soon. Why?" Chris shrugged his shoulders, "Well. . ." Leo said he thought she might be pregnant." "Chris the book of The Blood Moon said that male lycans are not ready to reproduce until the age of 25, so it would be impossible. Right?" Chris thought about it, "Well, that's the way it is in most cases, but sometimes, rarely, women do get pregnant." Kate thought about it but shrugged it off. She was happy for Jai and Leo. "So my love, what's the surprise for dinner?" Chris asked, wiping the soap off Kate's back. "Well, um . . . actually I was thinking about a big dinner, what do you think?" Chris thought about and agreed.

That night Jai and Kate made roast beef in Kate's kitchen. "So are you nervous?" Jai looked at Kate, pondering the question for a minute. "No not about telling everybody, or becoming a mother. I only hope Leo will be happy." Kate walked over to her and gave her a hug. "Don't worry Jai, he will be. Ready?" Jai nodded and they grabbed the food and started outside. Chris, Leo, Marcus, and Allision were all sitting at the table, candles around it giving it the perfect lighting. Kate sat down next to Chris, as Jai sat down next Leo. As everybody was making their plates and sitting down to eat, Jai stood up. "Everybody, I have an announcement to make. I am not sick; in fact, I'm pregnant, three months along." Leo stood up, eyes gleaming, "Really Jai? You're pregnant?" Jai shook her head. Leo jumped up, "Yes, I'm going to be a dad, I'm going to be a father!" Leo shouted. Everybody stood up and clapped their hands. Leo picked up Jai and gave her a hug and kiss, then leaned down by her stomach, "I love you, my child." He kissed her stomach. That night everybody was happy, especially Jai and Leo.

Chapter 10

The months went by fast. Kate and Jai learned how to knit blankets from Allision. Jai was showing, Kate even felt the baby kick a couple of times. Today was another doctor's appointment, except today was a special one, they was going to find out what the baby was. Kate and Leo have been taking turns going with Jai but today they both went. During the appointment Jai, Leo or Kate really didn't understand the ultrasound images, so they sat and listened as the doctor explained. He printed off a couple of pictures but only brought back one. He handed the picture to Jai and Leo. "Congratulations, Mr. and Mrs. Taylors, it's a boy, a very healthy boy." Jai started crying as she looked at the picture. Leo shook the doctor's hand and thanked him. All three of them were happy. Knowing what the baby was now, they decided to go shopping. Jai picked out a beautiful baby blue crib, as Leo bought a baby blue paint to paint the other room as a nursery. Kate bought a couple pairs of outfits. They packed the van and drove home.

Kate started to feel nauseous on the drive home. When Leo pulled into the driveway, Kate quickly jumped out of the van and started to vomit. Jai ran over to her, keeping her hair out of her face, as Kate was puking she felt a tingling sensation in her stomach, and then she disappeared right in front of Jai and Leo. Shocked they didn't know what to do, until they saw her leaning against a tree. Wiping her mouth she managed to say she was ok. Chris appeared, "Is everything ok?" Kate slowly stood up, "Yea, I guess I got a little car sick. Please help Jai and Leo with their bags; I'm going to take a shower." Chris nodded his head, kissed Kate's forehead and headed towards Jai and Leo. Kate headed the opposite way to the cabins.

After Chris and Leo carried their bags to Leo's cabin, Chris sat everything down. "I'm going to go check on Kate, I'll be back." Chris walked over to his cabin just as Kate was getting dressed. "Are you ok baby?" Kate wrapped her hair in a towel. "Yea Chris I feel better. I'm just going upstairs to take a little nap. I love you." Chris walked over to Kate and wrapped his arms around her. "Ok, well I'm going to help Leo get the baby's room ready. I heard it's a boy." Kate smiled "Yea, I'm happy for them." Chris kissed her forehead and led her upstairs to their room into the bed, he wrapped her in their blanket, and soon she was asleep. Chris returned to Jai and Leo's cabin. Leo already had half of the crib done, and Jai was putting away the clothes Kate bought.

Chris sat down by Leo who seemed to be having troubles. "So, any ideas for a name yet?" Jai turned to him, "We have a baby name book, we have a suggestions but nothing has stuck yet. How's Kate doing?" "She's fine, she took a shower and now she's sleeping." Jai nodded but both Chris and Leo sensed that she was worried. "Hey Jai, why don't you go visit Mark and Allision, so we can paint this room for you?" Chris asked. Jai smiled and was more than happy to go visit them. She walked past Kate's cabin and walked up to the porch of Marcus's and Allision's cabin. When she knocked on the door Marcus answered and with a smile on his face he was pleased to see Jai, he leaned in for a hug.

"Come in, Allision and I was just about to drink some tea, would you like to join us?" "Of course, thank you Mark." Jai replied with a smile. Jai walked in and sat down at the table. "So," Allision asked a little excited, "What did the doctors say?" Jai took a little drink before starting. "Well, they said the baby is doing great," Then Jai pulled out the ultrasound picture, "And it's also a boy. We're going to have a son!" They all three cheered.

Meanwhile back in Kate's bedroom, she was tossing and turning in her bed, dreaming. She was running down a road of trees, then a man stood there and then transformed into a wolf. "It's your time now Kate." Her hands started to glow red, with flames coming from them. Startled she woke up, smelling the smoke. Her hands quickly glowed blue putting the fire spots out. She jumped out of bed, looking it over, thankfully only the blanket was a little singed. She closed her eyes and thought about Chris.

When she opened her eyes she was in Marcus's and Allision's

cabin. Startled Allision jumped. "Mom, dad I'm so sorry. I was looking for Chris. Jai stood up, "He's at the cabin with Leo, is everything ok Kate?" "Yea, yea. So umm . . . what's for dinner?" Marcus looked at her confused but he didn't ask any questions. "Well, I was thinking we go into town, to celebrate Jai and Leo's upcoming son." Kate nodded and excused herself for a walk. Walking until she found a tree that covered the ground with shade, she sat down, thinking to herself. Chris said that it could happen but it she herself be pregnant as well? She disregarded the thought and returned to Chris and Leo.

Chris was painting, and Leo was hauling something that looked like a dresser. "Hey guys, need any help?" Chris shook his head but Leo nodded. "Sure, can you help me figure this thing out?" Kate laughed and sat down beside him.

Together they got the dresser up and it looked

great in a baby blue color. Soon, Marcus, Jai, and Allision came and got them, "You guys hungry?" All of them shook their heads. Chris and Leo changed and together they all went into town. Marcus treated them to a nice restaurant. After dinner they all went for a walk in town, stopping by the baby store, Kate bought Jai some extra clothes, a few packets of diapers, and wipes and bought this beautiful blue basket complete with everything the baby would need during and after a bath. Jai was overwhelmed with joy. That night Jai and Leo sat over with Kate and Chris. As the night got chilly Kate went to the fireplace, added the wood. Kate reached out her hand, first it glowed red then it changed to blue, the fire place was drenched with water. "Shit! Jai can you please come and help me?" Surprised Jai got up to help. Noticing the fireplace was wet as Kate was removing the wet boards and replaced them with dry boards. "Jai can you please set the wood on fire?" Jai did so but Kate walked away, sitting next to Chris.

Chris didn't want to ask any questions he didn't want the answers to. Trying to change the conversation and the tension in the room, Kate turned to Jai and Leo. "So any ideas for a name?" Jai and Leo looked at each other and said "Ian." Ian, Kate thought, what a nice name. Jai and Leo stayed over for a little longer before deciding it was time for bed. As Chris opened the door and led Jai and Leo out the door, Kate ran over to the bathroom, barley making it to the toilet, she started to vomit. Hearing Kate, Chris walked over to her, grabbed a wet towel and placed it on the back of her neck. "Kate, honey, is everything ok? You know you can tell me." She stood up, grabbed the rag and wiped her face. "Everything is fine, Chris. I'm going in town tomorrow to pick up some things, more stuff for baby Ian." Chris nodded his head and led Kate upstairs to their bedroom. That night Chris laid there, holding Kate, watching her as she slept.

Chapter 11

Kate went into town, nervous she arrived at the doctors. After filling out some forms, she sat down and waited. Finally a nurse came and called her name, still nervous she followed the nurse. They checked her weight, her blood pressure, and then led her into an examining room. Waiting it felt like forever until the doctor knocked on the door.

"Well, Mrs. Goshen, how's Jai doing?" it was the same doctor who was providing care for Jai's pregnancy. "She's fine doctor, I'm actually here for me." "Hmm, let me look over your charts." The doctor took a minute, and then asked Kate to provide a urine sample. Déjà Kate thought, but she did as the doctor asked. The doctor left and Kate waited for almost an hour. The doctor knocked once more and then opened the door, with a nurse following behind him with an ultrasound machine. Somehow Kate already knew the answer.

She lifted her shirt as the nurse rubbed the gel on her stomach, which was cold Kate thought. Just as Jai's first appointment, her' went the same, a peanut with a steady heartbeat, three months pregnant. That would explain the sickness and why her powers were going crazy. Now her only problem was telling everybody. She didn't want to take the attention away from Jai and Leo, they were so excited. So Kate decided to wait, she figured she could wear baggy clothes as she started to show.

After picking up her vitamins, she went back to the baby store, looking around at all the baby stuff made her happy in a sense. She picked up the stuff to make a baby pillow and a bay blanket. She figured it would be something to past the time. On her drive home, she almost couldn't believe she was pregnant, Chris said that it was rare but two times? To both Kate and Jai? Passing it through her mind, she grabbed her bags and placed the vitamins in her purse.

When Kate arrived in her cabin, everybody was there; they all looked as if they saw a ghost. Placing her bags on the ground, she asked "What's going on? What's wrong?" Marcus walked over to her and placed his hand on her shoulder. "Sir Taylors died. Late last night." Sir Taylors, Leo's father. Kate felt her heart drop. She went over to Leo. "Leo, I'm so sorry, I, I don't know what to say." Trying to keep back the tears that were whelming in his eyes, Leo looked at her, Thanks Kate. The funeral is the day after tomorrow. Everybody is expected."

That night was quiet as was the following day. Everybody kept to their selves. Kate and Chris checked on Leo every now and then but he never moved from the bed. That night the woods seemed even quieter than ever. Unable to sleep Kate went outside and sat at the picnic table, she sat there for a moment, until he mother came up behind her, wrapping her in a blanket, also handing her a nice hot cup of hot cocoa. "Couldn't sleep either?" Allision sat down beside her. "No mom, just thinking." Allision looked at her, "About becoming a mother? About when you are going to tell everybody?"

Surprised Kate quickly turned to Allision. "Tell who what?" Allision rubbed Kate's head. "Honey, a mother knows when her own daughter is about to become a mother herself." Kate looked down. "Mom, I didn't want anybody to know, Jai and Leo are so happy and now with Leo's father dying, that's the only thing they have to look forward to. I just didn't want anybody to know until the right time. Not yet mom." Allision continued to rub Kate's head, "When the times right you will know." Allison gave Kate a kiss on her forehead and walked back to her cabin. When the times right, when will it ever be right Kate thought.

Chapter 12

The next morning was dark and glomming, as usually it is before a funeral. In the middle of the speech, it started to rain, and got even darker. Kate knew that everybody there was either a lycan or a guardian. The man who gave the speech was tall, old, and wore complete black, but Chris and Leo knew right off it was the man from the council. After the tall man's eulogy of Sir Taylors, he offered Leo to come and say his own speech. Leo started to walk towards the podium, Jai offered him the umbrella but he declined. Walking up there he could tell everybody was feeling his pain, his grief, dark and cold, just how the day was. He approached the podium, drenching with rain, he turned and faced all the mourners. Leo really didn't know what to say but as he started it all seemed to fall into place.

"As you all know, my father was a great man. Being one of the 12 members of the council, he has protected the clans, as well as his family. When my mother passed away, I remember him promising me and my brothers will grow up knowing respect, honor, and greatness. I never told him but he was in fact all of these things and even more. I only wish I could be half the man my father was. I thank all of you for coming here today and paying your respect and honor. I'm sure my father would be proud. God bless his soul." As every word came out, Leo felt his voice get weaker and weaker, as his eyes got heavier and heavier. Leo bowed and left the podium.

As he was walking down the aisle of the graveyard, every man on both sides stood up and bowed to him, Leo kept his head up, trying not to show weakness. He returned to Jai's side and took her hand. As they lowered the dark casket, he held on tighter to Jai's hand, despite the pain, Jai allowed him to continue.

Slowly the crowd got smaller and smaller until only the six of them remained and the tall man who gave the speech in the beginning. He shook Marcus's hand and then made his way to Leo. "Mr. Taylors, I am so sorry for your lost. I want you to know that the whole clan is on the hunt for your fathers' killer. We suspect it was a rouge." Leo was surprised. His father never did anybody any harm, why would somebody kill him? Leo's heart felt like it was stone. As much as he was sad, he was also very angry, wishing more than anything he wished he knew who did this, killed his father, and why.

Marcus knew he was needed at the castle to help with the investigation. Therefore, he dropped off the two couples and Allision at the driveway and waited until he saw them disappear into the darkness. Once they were out of his sight he started to head towards the castle. As he entered, he saw the remaining 10 members of the council followed by other guards. They all sat in the main room, discussing what they found out. The tall man spoke first. "So far, we do know for a fact that it was a rouge who killed Sir Taylors. The question is, from which clan?" "Well the Veach clan was the only rouge clan close by but all of them are dead as far as we know. The five remaining clans are disqualified, but we still have nine more to consider, despite the fact that they are in different countries." Marcus stated. Then he started to remember, that night he and Allision saved Chris, quickly disregarding the idea, he knew that couldn't be possible. They sat there still talking about the possibilities until it became too late, and they all decided to leave and call it a night. Marcus returned to the cabin that night, falling asleep with many thoughts on his mind.

Chapter 13

The next morning Kate woke up early, dragging her feet, she went downstairs into the kitchen to make breakfast. Realizing there was no eggs, bacon, or anything for breakfast she decided to go to town.

Grabbing her purse and the keys, she didn't even mind going in her pajamas. Inside the store she bought eggs, bacon, and pancake mix. Then walking around just for a while she passed the baby store, which hasn't opened yet, she still couldn't believe she was going to be a mother. She felt like a child yet an adult all the same time. She returned to the van and drove home. Quietly she opened her door, tossing her purse on the floor she didn't realize her vitamins fell out. Cooking quietly, she heard Chris walking upstairs, then he appeared at the top of the stairs, smiling, making his way down the stairs.

"Well, well, well, something smells wonderful honey." Blushing, Kate smiled and sat Chris's plate on the table. Not paying attention to the food, Chris's eyes were fixed on Kate, somehow she had a glow on her. Coming up behind her he gave her a hug and a kiss on the cheek. "Good morning my love." "Morning." Kate turned around and wrapped her arms around him, slightly kissing him. "Juice, milk, or coffee honey?" Chris smiled. "Whatever you desire. You know Kate, us being married doesn't mean you have to act like my slave." "I know Chris, but it doesn't hurt cooking and trying new things, besides, I don't mind." Chris smiled again and turned to the table, with Kate behind him placing her plate next to his along with two cups of apple juice. They sat there and enjoyed their breakfast together. When they was done Kate started to clean up, as Chris sat there finishing his cup of juice.

"How do you this Leo is today?" Kate asked. Chris didn't say anything but shrugged his shoulders. "Maybe I'll go and check on him." Chris stood up and placed his cup in the sink, giving Kate a kiss he started towards the door. Noticing her purse was tipped over; Chris bent down to pick it up, also noticing a bottle of pills. "Prenatal vitamins. Kate Goshen. Take one a day." Surprised and shocked he turned to Kate, face to face, he placed the vitamins on the counter. "What are these Kate?" Sighing and cussing to herself, she knew she had to tell him.

"Chris I'm pregnant, three months along. I didn't want anybody to know because of Jai and Leo. I'm sorry." "Kate you should have told me, this is great! I'm going to be a father!" He ran up to her and gave her a slow and passionate kiss, then kissed her belly. "Kate this is wonderful. I love you." Kate smiled faintly, "I love you too Chris, but do you think we can keep this our secret, just for a little while?" Confused, Chris couldn't believe what he was hearing. "But Kate, this is the happiest day for me." Kate sighed again. "Ok, whatever you want my love." Chris immediately ran out the door.

Within minutes Marcus, Allision, and Jai were running inside with Chris leading them. He walked up behind Kate and rubbed her belly, "I'm going to be a dad!" Everybody cheered and clapped their hands. Marcus walked up to Chris, "Congratulations my son." Then he turned to Kate. "Kathern, I know you're young and probably wasn't expecting this just yet, I know you're scared but don't forget you have your whole family behind you, my princess." He gave her a kiss on her head. Noticing Leo wasn't in the room, Kate asked where he was. "He's still in bed. I don't think he will be getting out anytime soon." Jai said. "Oh, well I hope he will be ok." Kate said. Jai excused herself to return to Leo. As for Marcus and Allision, they stayed back, talking about the baby, how beautiful it was going to be, the powers the child can posse. Everybody was getting excited, except for Kate, she felt bad. She didn't want them to find out like this, or even today, the day after they buried Leo's father. Although she didn't know him, she still felt it necessary to grieve for him. Poor Leo was all Kate thought.

Chapter 14

    Time went by fast. Kate was now 6 months along and Jai was due any moment. Today was going to be the day that Kate and Leo finds out what the baby was. Chris wanted it to be a surprise but after felling the baby kick, he couldn't wait to get the nursery room ready. Kate was excited as well, picking out outfits, making blankets for the baby, she couldn't wait. Soon it was time for her appointment so everybody got in the van and drove to town. Leo finally gotten over the grieving period and he too was excited about his soon to be son. On the drive to town, Jai was constantly rubbing her side and holding her stomach.

    Concerned Leo turned to her and asked her what was wrong. "Oh nothing honey, cramps that all." She smiled to reassure him, however the pain was still sharp. They arrived at the doctors, with Chris going into the examining room with Kate, as Marcus, Allision, Jai, and Leo stayed back in the in the waiting room. The doctor asked a couple of questions and then the nurse came in with the ultrasound machine, Kate was so nervous she held Chris's hand the hold time while he sat next to her, never leaving his eyes from the screen. The doctor took a couple of pictures and printed them out. He looked them over and handed Kate a picture that had an arrow pointing to something that Kate couldn't make out, but there was an arrow pointing saying 'female'.

    The doctor shook Chris's hand. "Congratulations Mr. Goshen you're going to have a daughter." Chris stood up with happiness then kissed Kate, but she seemed to be in her own world. Looking at the picture, she couldn't believe she was going to have a daughter, her own little princess.

Tears started to fall down her cheeks, and right at that moment, she felt her daughter kick, her baby girl. Kate could already feel the protection wave falling over her. Chris helped Kate out of the chair and they walked to the waiting room where everybody was waiting. Marcus stood up first, as the rest followed. "So is it a prince or a princess?" Marcus asked. "It's a girl!" Kate shouted out. Allision and Jai ran up to her and hugged her, Jai telling her how happy she was for her. Allision stood there with tears in her eyes. "Honey, I'm so happy, I can tell this little girl is going to be special." Kate rubbed her stomach, "She already is mom."

Marcus declared that this was a time for a celebration. He treated everybody to a very nice restaurant. During the meal, Jai was constantly rubbing her side and her breathing started to get heavier and heavier. "So Kate, Chris, any names picked out yet?" Allision asked. Kate and Chris looked at each other. "Not yet Allision, but Jai allowed us to use her baby name book, we still haven't looked through it yet." Kate excused herself to go to the restroom; Jai excused herself as well and followed Kate.

Kate stepped out of the stall to go wash her hands, she saw Jai leaning against the wall, breathing very heavy, holding her stomach. Kate walked over to her, "Jai, Jai is everything ok? Are you alright?" "No, my side is killing me, Kate I think . . ." Before Jai could finish, Kate saw water running down Jai's legs. "Oh, shit, Jai you're going into labor. Stay here, just breathe. I'm going to get dad and Leo."

Quickly Kate ran out of the bathroom and ran to the table where everybody was sitting at. "Dad, Leo, Jai is going into labor, her water broke in the bathroom, you guys have to help her." Everybody jumped up from the table, plates chattering. "Allision get the van ready!" Marcus ordered as Leo and he ran to they ran to restroom, where they found Jai leaning against the wall, bent over. Leo wrapped one of his arms around his should as Marcus did the same on the other side of Jai. "Don't worry baby, Allision is getting the van, everything is going to be alright, just breathe." Leo was worried, scared but he tried so desperately trying to comfort both Jai and himself.

Kate was in the back seat with Allision in the driver's seat, as Chris held the door open for them. Marcus and Leo carefully slid Jai into the back seat, Leo and Marcus sitting with her as Chris quickly jumped in the passenger seat and Allision drove away. Allision flew down the streets trying to get to the hospital as quickly as she could; Jai was in the back breathing heavy as Leo rubbed her head. "Don't worry bay, I'm here for you, we're all here for you. I love you."

Love Lives Forever

They soon arrived at the hospital, and Chris and Allision jumped out the van and ran into the hospital. "We have a young lady in labor in the van, we need help now please!" Allision yelled getting every nurse and doctors attention. Soon a nurse came with a wheelchair. Leo and Marcus were slowly sliding Jai out of the van. They helped her into the wheelchair as she was rubbing her stomach; she started to scream out in pain.

Leo filled out all the papers the doctor needed. The doctor asked who was the father and Leo quickly stated he was. "Mr. Taylors, would you like to go in the delivery room with Jai?" "Yes, yes please." The doctor allowed Leo to scrub up and soon he was beside Jai, holding her hand and wiping her forehead with a sponge. Jai yelled out in pain as the doctor was examining her. "Alright Mrs. Taylors, I need you start pushing, the baby is ready."

Jai took in a deep a breath and pushed, yelling at the same time. "Jai, you are doing a great job, I can see the head, but I need you push one more time, hard please?" The doctor asked. Jai nodded her head, took in another deep breath and started to push, yelling even louder, Leo standing next to her. "Baby, you're doing great, soon we will have our son." "Alright here we go, one, two, and three . . ." Suddenly a baby's cry filled the room, Jai fell back in the chair with relief.

"It's a boy, congratulations. Mr. Taylors, would like to cut the cord?" "Yes, yes of course, please." The nurse took the baby and cleaned him up, weighing him, and took foot prints and finger prints. Then the nurse wrapped him up in a blanket and handed him to Jai, with dark hair, to Jai he was a vision from heaven. The doctor turned to Leo, "Sir, what's the baby's name?" Leo held his head up proud, "Ian, Ian Taylors." Leo walked over to Jai, watching his newborn son. "Honey you did great, wonderful. Look at him, he's so beautiful. I love you Jai." Leo gave Jai a kiss on her lips and in a whisper, she said "I love you too Leo." Jai looked back down at baby Ian, admiring his features, she whispered in his ear, "I love you Ian." Looking at him, Jai felt like she finally accomplished something right for once in her life.

For the next three days, Kate and Chris never left, Jai, Leo, or Ian's side. Taking turns Chris and Kate, brought them all clean clothes and homemade food. Marcus was standing outside the hospital doors, waiting for Jai and Ian's release. As Leo walked out holding Ian, Jai was being wheeled out by a nurse. Marcus gracefully held Jai in the van as Leo strapped Ian in his car seat. Jai and Leo sat in the backseat together holding hands, admiring the miracle they made together. Marcus pulled into the drive way, with Chris waiting for them to help. "Where's Kate?" Jai asked as Chris helped her out of the van. "She's back at the cabins, there's really not much she could help with here."

Slowly and carefully they finally made their way to Jai's and Leo's cabin. When they opened the door, Kate was there standing in the middle of the living room. Quietly, she said "Surprise!" holding up her hands, where there was a banner that said 'WELCOME HOME BABY IAN' in a baby blue color. On the table there was fresh cooked food and on the counter was three bags tied together with blue ribbons.

Blushful Jai smiled. "You guys, you didn't have to go through all this trouble." Marcus came up behind her and wrapped his arm around her shoulder. "Nonsense, you're family Jai, and we treat family how they should be treated." Tearfully Jai smiled and hugged Marcus and Allision. "Come on Jai, we got you and Ian some presents." Jai sat down next to Leo as Allision held Ian. Kate handed Jai the first bag, "This one is from mom and dad, mom mainly." Jai opened the bag and pulled out a basket, containing bath beads, moistening lotion, perfume, a cute pink pouf, and some hair ties. Jai smiled, "Thank you Mark, Allision. This is so wonderful." Allision smiled, "Becoming a new mother, you deserve a nice gift to relax when you want to."

Kate handed Jai the next bag. "This one is from all of us." Jai opened the bag; she pulled out three new outfits and a picture of Leo and Jai when she was still pregnant. Jai laughed at the picture. "Thank you." Kate handed her the last bag. "Before you open it, I had to go through your baby stuff just to see if you had one. So when I saw you didn't, I couldn't help myself, I made it by hand." Jai looked at Kate, a little confused but she still opened the bag. She pulled out a blue book; flipping through the pages she realized it was a baby book. "the picture of you and Leo, that's suppose to go on the front page where it says 'MOMMY AND DADDY' but you don't have to use that picture. I know it's a little corny but . . ." Jai jumped up and gave Kate a huge hug. "Thank you so much Kate, its perfect." Kate looked at her. "Jai, you are like my sister, and I don't ever want you to forget that. I'll always be here for, we all will be. Like dad said, you're family." The two shared a long hug.

Allision, Kate and Chris made plates for everybody and they sat and enjoyed their meal, together as a family. Allision took a couple of pictures of everyone, and then sat the timer on the camera and they all posed together, smiling as a family.

Chapter 15

Life with Ian was wonderful, three months old; nobody knew how fast he would grow. Jai and Leo were so proud; they constantly took pictures of Ian. Kate was now 9 months pregnant, prepared for everything for their upcoming daughter. Kate and Chris still haven't picked out a name yet, but they had a couple ideas picked out but only one stuck out to Kate, Carmen. Everybody was invited to a dinner, they sat there eating, laughing, and enjoying themselves until there was a knock at the door.

Not expecting anybody, everybody was surprised, nobody knew where they lived. Then the knock came again. Marcus stood up and opened the door, but this, nobody expected. "Jai, Kate, take Ian upstairs and lock the door. Leo, Chris, Allision come here now." You couldn't see much of the man, covered in black, with a black cloak on, but through the darkness, they could see his eyes, red, a rouge.

The stranger spoke. "May I come in please?" "No. State your reasoning for being here, now." Marcus spoke like the king he was once before. The stranger removed his hood, everybody gasped, not only for the burns that covered half of his face, neck and maybe even more, but it was the other side of his face, he looked just like Chris, identical. Confused Chris had to sit down, this can't be happening, not now. The stranger spoke again. "What's the matter Chris? Did you forget about me? You're twin bother?!" Eyes glowing even more red. Chris never knew he had another bother, especial a twin brother. He was raised in the Tipo Castle and when it came time the maids and guards told him about his father and Cole but not this.

"I know we are on different teams brother, however allow me to introduce myself. My name is Matt Veach, the last remaining member of the Veach clan, other than you, brother." Chris stood up, "You are not my brother. My name is Chris Goshen, and I am ordering you to leave now!" "Tst, tst, tst brother, I only came to welcome my niece and my sister in law, and besides, I did say please." Eyes glowing, Chris started to charge towards Matt, but Marcus and Leo restrained him.

"You keep away from my family, I mean it!" Matt laughed. "Oh, but I'm not done yet. Leo I heard they are still looking for your father's killer." Leo tensed up, but tried not lose control. Matt continued, "Well, today must be your luck day. I am here to confess. I was the one who killed your father. What are you going to do now Leo?" Leo released Chris and he started towards Matt until Marcus stopped him. "Leo, son, do you really want to fight now? With your wife and newborn son upstairs. There will be another day. Think about it, this could end up very bad." Matt clapped his hands, "He's right Leo, for all you know, I could kill every single person in this pathetic cabin, and not even break a sweat." Marcus stood in between them, facing Leo, "He's right Leo, there will be another day and time, but right now you have to think about your family, your son."

Leo knew he was right so he backed down, sitting in one of the chairs. Matt turned to Chris, "As for you brother, your time will come, and as for your little princess, she will be mine." Then eyes growing that usual red, he vanished. Chris never knew about him having another brother, a twin at that. Marcus and Allision sat down and explained to Chris, that when they rescued him, there was another baby's cry, but by the time Allision reached the doors, the cries stopped, they figured it was too late. Knowing all of this now, Chris knew his family was no longer safe. That night Chris went to sleep worried, holding Kate as close as he could.

The next morning Kate woke up as usual to make breakfast, as she was making the plates she saw Chris walk down the stairs. "Good morning baby." He kissed her and headed towards to the bathroom. Hearing the shower running, she decided to surprise Chris.

She knocked on the door. "Chris, honey, breakfast is ready." Through the door he replied, "Ok baby, I'm almost done." She stood there for a minute longer then knocked once more. "Umm Chris, do you mind if

I join you?" Although she couldn't see it, she could feel he was smiling. "Of course my love." She opened the door and took off her clothes and entered the shower with Chris. Despite what Kate thought about her body, Chris knew she was the most beautiful creature he has ever seen. Rubbing her back, Chris made Kate feeling relaxed. Not wanting to cut their shower off early, but Kate reminded Chris of their breakfast ready. "Of course. Ladies first." Chris helped Kate caustically out of the shower. She dried off and handed Chris the towel as she got dressed. She left the bathroom and returned to the kitchen, Chris soon followed.

They sat down and started to eat, but there were other things on Kate's mind, and before she thought, she spoke. "Who was the vaster last night honey?" Disappointed about the conversation, Chris put down his fork. "Until last night, I only knew of my brother Cole, I learned that from the guards and maids at the castle. I didn't, I didn't know I had another one. I was so young, I don't even remember. The visitor from last night, his mane is Matt, Matt Veach. He's my twin brother. And he's going to try to do what Cole tried to accomplish. He is also the one who killed Leo's father." Kate just looked at Chris, worry flushing over her eyes. "Honey I know you love this place, but we all agreed that once when the baby is born, we should move to Minnesota, where you're from. It will be safe there." Kate grew furious, angry, worried, all the emotions at once. Kate stood up to take her plate to the sink. Chris still sitting at the table, hearing glass breaking he walked over to the kitchen. "Kate, Kate, honey are you ok?" He walked over past the counter and he saw Kate, on the floor, water on the floor, followed by blood. He quickly ran over to her, yelling for help.

Marcus, Allision, and Leo ran in the cabin. Allision ran over to Kate.

"Her water has broken and she is starting to bleed out, Leo I need you to get some clean water, towels and blankets. She going into labor and she's going to have the baby here now." Leo quickly returned with what Allision asked for. "Chris I need you to place her head on your lap, holding both of her hands. This is going to be very painful for her; you need to be here for her. Leo bring me the water and towels." Quickly Leo took the water and towels over to Allision.

She placed the towels under Kate, wiping her head, "Kate, honey, I need you to stay with me ok?" Hazily, Kate nodded. "Marcus, find some alcohol and a pair of succors, this has to be done clean." Everybody followed Allision's orders, as if she knew exactly what she was doing.

111

"Ok Kate, I need you to give me a push, as hard as you can." From losing all the blood Kate felt very weak, and as if her body was being drained, but she pushed as hard as she could. "Nothing yet Kate, honey I need you to push again, this time harder. I know it hurts but you have to try honey." Kate held Chris's hands, pushed and screamed, loud enough that it echoed through the cabin. "Good job Kate, I can see her head, but . . . the cord looks as if it's wrapped around her neck. I need you to push one more time, harder, as hard as you can." Quickly Kate pushed harder, breathing hard. "There she is, keep going, almost there. Here she comes."

Quickly Allision unwrapped the cord from the baby's neck, but she didn't make a sound. Chris ran over to Allision and the baby, holding his hands over her, they glowed green, he tried harder then suddenly a cry came from the baby. "Kate she's alive, Kate she's . . ." Chris turned to Kate who laid on the floor passed out, even more blood flowing on the floor. "She's losing blood quickly; we have to get her to the hospital right away." They carefully carried Kate to the van as Chris held the baby. They quickly arrived at the emergency room and rushed Kate into an operation room, while Chris filled out the paperwork and a nurse took the baby and under the name he placed "Carmen Goshen."

Marcus, Allision and Chris sat and waited for three hours before the doctor finally came out. "Mr. Goshen, your wife will be fine. She has lost a lot of blood, when her water broke the baby pushed through the placenta and tore Mrs. Goshen inside. Right now she is resting, but you are more than welcome to visit her now. The nurses are checking over your daughter right now, so far everything looks great, she's as healthy as a horse." Both Chris and Marcus stood up to shake the doctor's hand. Chris stayed to walk to Kate's room, and then he saw the baby nursery, without even asking he already knew which one was his. There she was, cuddled in a pink blanket with a little cute pink hat, with a face just like her mothers.

Chris continued to walk towards Kate's room until he came to it, with the door shut, he looked at the tag on the door, "Goshen, Kathern." Chris knocked on the door but without a response he opened the door. A nurse was in the room, checking Kate's vitals. He sat down on her bed, holding her hand. The doctors kept a very close eye on Kate for the next three days, on the third day they released Carmen under the care of Marcus and Allision while Chris stayed by Kate's side at all times. A week's time has passed when the doctor knocked on her door. "Mrs. Goshen, I hope you're feeling better. Mr. Goshen."

Kate sat up in her bed, "Yes doctor, much better. Thank you." The doctor nodded and leaned over Kate to check her vitals. Until now she never paid attention to the doctor's name, he never mentioned it. Reading his name tag it said "Dr. Forestry, M." "Ok, Kate everything seems to be fine. I'll go sign the release papers now and within a few hours you will be out of here and home with your newborn." Kate shook his hand, as well as Chris "Thank you doctor. You've done a great job."

Chris called Marcus and after a few hours of packing and signing papers, Kate and Chris were out the door. The ride home was long and quiet, and Kate was already feeling pains running down her stomach to her pelvis. They arrived at the cabins driveway; Chris helped Kate to their cabin only to find Allision holding Carmen. Before settling down and unpacking, Kate as ked to speak to Chris privately. They walked upstairs and Kate shut the door behind them. "Chris, the doctor, did you happen to catch his name?" Chris knew where she was getting at with this. "Yeah, Michal Forestry. He is one of the clans' masters. Their clan mainly posses the powers of nature, thus their name Forestry." Kate just stared at him, slightly confused, "So he knew who we were? What we are?" "Of course. That's why he took such great care of you." Chris stated. "Oh, ok well we will have to send him a thank you card soon." Kate suddenly felt wet down below, looking down; she noticed blood bleeding through her pants. "Shit, Chris do you mind getting me a pair of jeans and underwear?" Kate quickly ran down the stairs to the bathroom. Jumping in the shower she quickly washed off, Chris came in to bring her the clean clothes she asked for, and sat down on the toilet. "You know Kate, now that Carmen is born and is here safe, maybe we should leave, all of us, back to Minnesota, like we talked about. It would be safer. Please?" Kate turned off the shower and started to dry off, recalling what Chris said, about his brother Matt. Getting dressed, Kate turned to Chris. "Let's start packing."

Part Three

Part Three

Chapter 1

~16 YEARS LATER~

"*N*o one in the world knows how werewolves came to be. They world doesn't even know if they really exist, but I do. My name is Carmen Goshen, daughter of Kathern and Chris Goshen. And this, this is my story now. All my life my parents have taught me who I am, who I will be. Last night I had the dream and today, on my 16th birthday, under the blood moon, I will change, that is my choice."

Carmen laid down her journal as she finished writing. She knew exactly what to expect tonight, thanks to her mother and father for not keeping any secrets from her about who she is. Carmen knew everything. She grabbed her bag and started downstairs. As expected her mother and father was sitting at the table. Kate sat straight up, "So . . . ?" Carmen grabbed her coat and turned around, brown hair with natural blonde highlights, swinging around, and her green eyes glowing even brighter. "I'll be here, say around eleven? I love you both. Bye." Carmen walked out the door of their cozy little house. In the driveway stood Ian Taylors, waiting by his car. Since the day Carmen turned 13, they've been dating, and with no doubt, she knew she loved him.

With arms opened wide, his handsome smile and green eyes that just seemed to sparkle every day, Carmen ran into his arms. Ian kissed the side of her head, "Happy birthday and happy anniversary baby." He pulled out a big pick bag that said happy birthday on it. Carmen opened the bag and pulled out a beautiful pink purse with a bright red rose that sparkled. The vine wrapped all the way around the back, and even the strap had a vine going around it. Carmen was surprised at how much detail was put into it. "Thank you Ian, it's beautiful." Ian smiled, "Well thank you, but that's just the first gift. Here's the other one." Ian pulled out a small box from his pocket. When he opened it there was a gold ring with a green gem inside it. "Ian, you didn't have to . . ." Ian stopped her in the middle of her sentence. "Carmen I love you, I've always have, but just for now, let's call this a promise ring, until I can get you a real one." He handed her the ring. "Read what's engraved on the inside." Reading inside the ring were the words "Love Lives Forever—Ian" Carmen smiled. "I love you Ian." Ian smiled as he opened the door for Carmen. "Shall we go to school my love?" "Yea, why not?" Ian jumped in the driver's seat and started the car and headed towards school.

"So what are you going to choose?" Ian asked so curiously and excited. Carmen smiled without looking at him, "What do you think?" Ian laughed. "So your place at eleven?" "It's a date." They arrived at school and did just like any other day. Go to their classes; go to lunch at the dinner down the road, returned to school to finish their classes and once when that final bell rang they were out the doors. Before getting in the car, Ian stopped Carmen. "Since you are deciding to change, I got something else for you." He reached into the conical of his car and pulled out another box, bigger than the ring box. When he opened it there was a golden charm bracelet with three charms on it, two of them were wolves with a green diamond as the eyes. The last charm was a white rose with a red diamond in the middle of it. Carmen smiled and gave Ian a kiss.

"Hey mom's going to be making dinner tonight, why don't you come over?" Ian smiled "That would be great but dad wants me to help him work on the car. I'm sorry baby. But I promise I will be there at ten, ok?" Carmen was a little disappointed but she smiled and agreed. Ian drove Carmen home, gave her a kiss and promised again that he would be there by ten. Carmen walked into her house, with Kate already starting on dinner. "Hey mom, how was your day?" Carmen walked over to Kate and gave her a hug. "Good. How was yours honey?" "It was great. Ian got me a couple of presents." Carmen showed her mom all the things that Ian got her. "Oh honey, that's s o sweet. So . . . you guys are getting serious?"

Carmen looked at her mom, "Yea, I love him mom, I know I'm young, but I think he's the one for me." Kate smiled, "You remind me so much of myself." "Do you need help with dinner?" Kate looked around, "Sure honey, if you don't mind." "Not at all mom." Roast beef, dads favorite Carmen thought. Right before dinner, Chris came home. Carmen ran up to him and gave him a hug. "Hi daddy, how was work?" Chris smiled and gave her a kiss on her forehead. "It sucked, like any other day at the factory, but when I come home and see my little princess, it makes my day so much better." Carmen smiled. Kate was going through the cabinets. "Chris, honey, I know you just got home, but I forgot to pick up some cake mix, do you mind going to the store for me?" Chris smiled. "Sure baby, I needed to stop by Jai's and Leo's place anyways." Chris left just as quickly as he came home.

Kate and Carmen sat the table with their food and then waited. It was only about five minutes to the store and ten to Jai's and Leo's house, Kate started to worry, she hopped everything was ok. The clock ticked by and it was already eight when Chris came running through the door, with his shirt ripped and covered in blood, pants bloody as well. Kate jumped up, "Oh my god Chris! What happened?" Kate grabbed a rag and started to wipe him down but he pushed her hand away. "Jai, Leo, and Ian were attacked, we have to get over there fast, Jai's hurt so bad she can't heal anybody even herself." All three jumped in their car and Marcus drove quickly to get there. As they pulled into the driveway, Kate and Carmen quickly jumped out of the car and ran inside.

The house was destroyed, the door broken off the hinges, windows broken with the pictures scattered on the floor, the couch thrown in pieces, and the TV knocked over broken. Carmen followed the blood spots that led into the main room where Leo and Jai laid on the floor, Ian sitting next to them. All three were covered in blood and scratches. "Dad, what happened here?" Chris looked at Kate and then looked at Carmen.

"A rouge. Come on we have to help them." Ian looked at Chris, "Mr. Goshen, please tell me you can help them." Chris looked at them then kneeled down, Kate kneeling beside Chris, holding hands, they each held out their other hand. Glowing green and blue, Carmen and Ian watched as the wounds healed. Slowly Jai and Leo sat up, rubbing their heads, their shirts were torn up. Kate went over to Ian to heal him, as Carmen held his hand. "Mom, who did this? And why?" Chris asked Carmen to leave the room so they could talk. Carmen left and went outside for some fresh air. Checking her cell phone, it was almost nine, if she didn't change tonight, she would never get to change, only take the powers of her parents.

Back in the house in the room, all five of them sat on the bed. "It was him Chris, he has come back to finish his business. I don't know how he found us, but he's not going to stop." Leo held Jai's hand as he spoke. Chris stood up, rubbing his hand through his hair. "Carmen is not to know about this. Jai, Leo, and Ian, start packing. We are going back to the castle. We will meet with Mark and Allision and figure what to do from here." The Taylors all nodded and started to pack. Chris sat down by Kate. "And Carmen? Chris, if she doesn't change tonight . . ." "I know Kate, she's next to being princess of the Tipo Clan, but if she doesn't, she can be a guardian. Maybe that's the best for her. You and your father can run the clan." Kate thought about it, she only wanted what was best for her daughter. Kate got up and helped Jai pack. Chris went outside to meet with Carmen.

"Carmen, there's something we need to talk about." Both Carmen and Chris sat down on the porch. "Carmen I understand you want to change, and to me that's an honor. But your mother and I think it would be better, for your own safety, to be only a guardian. There are dangers lurking around, and so we are going to leave, us and the Taylors. We are returning to the Tipo Castle." Carmen couldn't believe what she was hearing. All her life she was told, she was taught to do this, to change, to carry on the family name, but now everything's changing, and Carmen knew better not to disagree, especially with her father. "Ok dad, I'll do whatever you need me to do." Relieved that she wasn't arguing Chris grabbed Carmen and held her tight. "Let's start packing honey, let's leave here."

Chapter 2

As they drove up to the Tipo Castle, Carmen couldn't believe how big it was. Guards were already at the gates to greet them. As Kate, Chris, and Carmen walked up the stairs, the guards bowed, "Welcome back Princess Kathern." Carmen has no idea how important her mother was here. Two large guards opened the doors to the castle. And there they stood, Mr. and Mrs. Marcus Tipo, Carmen's grandparents. Allision held out her arms, "Carmen, my darling." Carmen ran up to her. "Grandma, I've missed you so much. And you too grandpa." Marcus smiled, "As well for us Carmen." Chris walked to them. "Mark, Allision, a pleasure as always. Marcus do you mind sending a guard to watch over Carmen?" "Not at all." Marcus summoned a guard, "Yes my Lord?" Marcus turned to Carmen. "This is my granddaughter, I need you to watch over her." The guard bowed. "Yes my Lord, of course." The guard turned to Carmen, "Miss Goshen, I am here to protect to you." Carmen turned to Chris. "Dad I don't need a guard, I have Ian to watch over me." "But Carmen, this guard . . ." Marcus turned him. "No Chris its fine, if Carmen prefers Mr. Ian to watch over her, that's fine." "Very well." "Thank you grandpa." Carmen said with a smile on her face.

"Dad, can Ian and I go outside to the garden?" Knowing that the adults needed to talk alone, Chris gave her the permission. Carmen quickly grabbed Ian's hand and they ran outside. Marcus asked everybody to meet in the library. Soon the library was filled with all the adults. Chris spoke first, "Mark, the Taylors were attacked last night at their home." Marcus looked at Jai and Leo and could still smell the fresh blood that lingered on their bodies. "Do we know who did this?"

Leo spoke then, "Yes, it was Matt, Matt Veach; we believe he's here to finish what he started 16 years ago." "We have to keep Carmen safe; our best bet is to keep her here at the castle. We can have around the clock guards watching over her. And guards need to be constantly watching the doors." Kate noted. Everybody agreed. Marcus made the orders.

Marcus arranged for Kate and Chris to have a room, Jai and Leo a room, Ian had his own room, and right next to his was Carmen's room, with two guards to be guarding the door.

Meanwhile Carmen and Ian were outside in the garden. Ian had already changed three months ago so he posses the power of fire, but Carmen couldn't help but wonder if she even going to ever get her own powers. "You know, honey, I can read your mind, and yes, even though you won't change, you will still posse either all or at least one of the powers from your parents."

They held hands and walked until Carmen noticed a bench, and she sat down. Now Ian was confused. "Baby what's wrong?" Ian asked sincerely, grabbing her hand. "Something's not right Ian, your family being attacked and now all of a sudden they want us to come here? Plus, I feel like somebody's watching me." Nobody noticed or even saw, but in the back, in a corner, sat a dark figure, eyes glowing red. Noticing Carmen starting to shiver, Ian took off his jacket and wrapped it around Carmen, and suggested that they go back inside.

As they opened the doors, the smell of food filled their nostrils, but Carmen wasn't the least bit hungry.

Chris came and greeting them. "Hey, how was your walk kids?" "Fine dad." Hearing the tension in her voice, he knew better to ask, he already knew what was wrong. "Ok, well dinner is almost ready." "Dad, I'm not hungry, I would just rather go and take a shower and go to bed, please?" Chris thought for a moment. "Ok sweetie, I'll have a guard escort you to your room." "No dad, I rather have Ian walk me to my room." Carmen grabbed Ian's hand and started to walk up the stairs. They reached Carmen's room, "Well good night baby." Carmen said. "Good night." Ian leaned in and gave Carmen a kiss on her lips, and suddenly felt a spark. Ian waited until Carmen shut the door. He knew soon she would start getting her powers.

Carmen walked into her room, her bags sat next to her bed. She went through her bags until she found a pair of pajama pants and a shirt, she also found her travel bag. She opened the door the bathroom and started the shower. Carmen got undressed and jumped in the shower. She washed her hair, and then sank down; she sat there, water flowing over her. Something wasn't right, she didn't even feel like herself anymore, suddenly she felt lost. Carmen got out of the shower, got dressed, and went to lie down. Right as she turned to turn off the light on her nightstand, there was a knock on her door. When Carmen opened the door, there stood Kate with a bag. "Carmen, can I come in?" "Uh, yea sure mom." Kate walked in and sat down on the bed, patting the bed for Carmen to come and sit with her.

Carmen sat down next to her, wondering what she was going to say. "Listen Carmen, I know how much you wanted to change, but being a guardian isn't all that bad, you know your grandmother is a guardian. But I'm not here to preach to you, I'm here to give you this." She opened the bag and pulled out a book. "This was pasted on to me on my 16th birthday, and now, it belongs to you. It's the Book of the Blood Moon. This explains everything else that we didn't explain to you. I want you to read it, look it over. It will help." Carmen took the book and held it in her hands. "Thanks mom, I'll um, look it over." "Ok, I love you, my princess." Kate kissed Carmen on her forehead and left. Once when her door was shut, Carmen opened the book, but then decided she didn't even want to look at it. "Princess? I'm not a princess. I never was." Carmen said to herself. She sat the book on the side table, turned around in her bed and went to sleep.

Chapter 3

Carmen woke up with a knock on her door. Before she could open it, Ian walked in carrying a plate of food. "Good morning beautiful, I thought I should surprise you with breakfast in bed." "Aww, thanks baby." Carmen was so happy to see him. She scooted across the bed making room for Ian to sit down next her. Carmen started to eat when Ian noticed the book on her side table. "Hey, the book of the Blood Moon. Have you read it yet?" shaking her head Carmen replied, "No, besides what's the point? I didn't change."

Ian looked at her. "Carmen, just because you didn't change, does not mean you're not special. Come on, finished eating and we'll go to the garden and we can read through it together. Yea?" Despite how much she didn't want to go, she did want to spend time with Ian, so she agreed. Once when Carmen finished eating, she got dressed, braided her hair. When she came out of the restroom, Ian was waiting for her with the book in one hand, and holding out his other hand, Carmen took it and they walked down the stairs to the main doors. Ian gracefully opened the door for her and they held hands and walked to the garden.

Passing the bench they sat on last night, Carmen noticed a huge beautiful tree that covered the ground with shade; she thought that would be perfect. Carmen dragged Ian to the tree, and they sat down and leaned against the tree, Ian wrapped one arm around Carmen's shoulder as she opened the book. To her nothing interested her, until she came to the part of the Pure White, reading over it, it somehow connected to her. As she flipped through the pages, it started to fascinate her even more, until she saw the picture, the picture of her grandfather. Then there was a note stuck to the side of the page.

> "My name is Kathern Tipo, Princess of the Tipo Clan. My father, Marcus Tipo, is the Pure White, the first of the lycans. There has never been another Pure Whit, until now. On the night of my 16th birthday under the blood moon, I changed, changed into the next Pure White."

"Ian, my mom is the pure white! She posses all the powers a lycan can. Do you think... I could have all the powers as well?" Ian thought about then got an idea. "Well, when dad taught me to transform, he said to just feel it, think it, then you get this tingling sensation in your stomach. That's how you know it happens." Carmen looked at the book, the picture of her grandfather, the note from her mother. "May we can try something, something small." Ian looked around then picked up the book. "What about trying to use the power of earth? It says here you can bloom flowers, trees, even mountains. You wanna try Carmen?" Nervously Carmen shook her head, "Yea, why not?" Ian smiled, "Ok baby, hold out your hand, and think about a flower, a rose."

Slowly and shaking, Carmen held out her hand, she closed her eyes and thought about a rose, how beautiful they look, suddenly she got a tingling sensation not only in her stomach, but through her whole entire body. Ian watched as her whole body glowed a vibrant green color. When Carmen opened her eyes she saw not only one, but a whole dozen of beautiful, perfect white roses. Surprised Carmen jumped back, forgetting Ian was behind her, pushing him into the tree. "Shit, did you see that? Did I do that?" Ian looked at her, with wide eyes and a very surprised look on his face. "Yeah, you did that. You did it baby!" Carmen jumped up, as happy as she could be. Ian picked her up and swung her around. "You did it baby, you did! I'm so proud of you!" Carmen smiled, "Come on, let's go show everybody." Carmen grabbed the roses and Ian's hand and quickly they ran to the castle.

Chapter 4

As Carmen and Ian entered the castle, Marcus, Allision, Chris, Kate, Jai, and Leo all sat together in a circle reading a letter, fear over their faces. "Mom, dad, what's wrong?" Carmen sat down next to her mom and dad, Ian still standing. Marcus put down the letter. "There has been another attack; the entire council has been killed." "What do you mean? Who attacked them?" Carmen looked around, she felt as if everybody knew something she didn't, even Ian. "Well? Who did it?!" Carmen slammed her hands on the table, the roses following to pieces on the ground. Everybody stared at her. "Carmen, why don't you go to your room, please?" Kate looked at her, Carmen returning the look. "Fine!" Carmen slammed her hands on the table again and started up the stairs with a guard following her. Carmen turned around, "Do not follow me!" She faced the guard, her eyes and hands glowing green. The guard quickly turned around and walked back down the stairs. Walking up to her room, Carmen slammed the door.

"It was him, it's Matt. He has found us, and he wants to kill us, he has made that clear." Marcus looked at everybody. "Ian, please go and calm down Carmen. And Ian, do not speak a word about this to her." Ian stood up, "Yes sir." Ian started to walk towards the stairs. "And Ian," Ian turned around. "Yes sir?" "Keep her safe." Ian nodded, "Yes sir."

Ian started up the stairs and got to Carmen's door. He knocked, but no answer. As he reached out his hand to knock once more Carmen opened the door. "Carmen, baby, can I come in please?" Carmen stood there, arms crossed. Looking at Ian made Carmen open the door more, allowing Ian to enter. Ian sat down on the bed; Carmen shut the door, turning around facing Ian, arms still crossed.

"Ian, everybody is hiding something, and I think you know something about it. Now I want you to explain it to me, please?" Ian sighed. "Listen Carmen, I can't explain anything expect there is somebody going around killing off the clans. All we want to do is keep you safe. So please just listen to whatever anybody tells you to do. It's for your best." Carmen looked at him eyes glowing green. "I'm so tired of everybody telling me what's best for me. You know more, Ian. Why can't you just tell me?!" "Because I'm protecting you!" "From who?!" Both Ian and Carmen stopped yelling, Ian looked at her, he couldn't lie to her anymore. He sighed and sat on the bed.

"Carmen, his name is Matt Veach, he is a rouge, and he is trying to
kill the whole family." "Why?" Carmen asked, sitting next to him, gazing in his eyes. "Because, well, he wants to get revenge, on your father." "Why? What did my dad do to him?" Ian sighed again, rubbing his hands over his face. ""Matt's father attacked your mother, almost killed her, well, in fact, he did kill her. It was a miracle that your father was able to bring her back. Carmen, Matt is your father's brother, his twin brother, Matt is your uncle. He is very evil and very strong." Carmen stood up taking in all the information Ian had just told her. Suddenly she felt anger flush over her, her body glowing a bright green. "You knew? About all of this? And you didn't even have the decently to tell me?! Your girlfriend? I can't change, I've lost the only thing I was taught to do, the only thing I had to look forward too, and now it's gone. And you. You were just going along with all of this, this plot to keep everything from me. You lied to me Ian!" Ian stood up, "It was all to protect you! You don't know everything Carmen and it's best if you don't." "And because of you, because of everybody . . ." Ian started to walk over to Carmen but she pushed him away.

"Don't you dare touch Ian Taylors; get away from me, now! Leave, get the fuck out of my room! And don't even think about talking to me again!" Carmen screamed at him. She walked over to the door and opened it. Ian started to walk towards her. "I said get out now!" Ian didn't move, Carmen pushed him towards the door, knocking him out of the door with such a force, Ian couldn't control. Slamming the door in his face, Ian stood at the door, hands bracing the door frame.

"Carmen, please open the door." He didn't hear an answer, anything, he waited for a minute. "Ok, Carmen, open the door, now please."

Suddenly Ian heard Carmen scream. "Marcus, Chris, Guards!!" Ian yelled out as he was pushing the door, finally pushing it open, Marcus and Chris was right behind him. Standing in the room by the window, Matt was holding onto Carmen by her hair, with the other arm wrapped around her neck.

"Matt, let her go, she has nothing to do with this." Chris walked passed Marcus and Ian, standing guard. "Chris, Chris, Chris. She has everything to do with this, she is the next heir to the throne, and once when all of you are dead, and she's dead, this pathetic little clan will be over. Soon I will be king, and the new clan will be run by me, the pathetic little humans in this world will know fear." "Matt, don't this." Matt looked at Chris, eyes glowing red. "Too late brother." He jumped out of the window, taking Carmen with him. Marcus, Ian, and Chris ran to the window. "Carmen!" Chris yelled out. Hearing Carmen's screams slowly drifting away, they all watch as they disappeared in the woods.

Chapter 5

Carmen woke up, tied to a chair with her hands behind her. Her vision was blurry, until it started to come back. She could see that it was dark, extremely dark, besides the few candles that were lit. She couldn't tell, but it looked as if she was in a cellar or a basement. Carmen wiggled her arms but it was no use, the rope was tied too tight for her to loosen them up. "Don't try to get lose Miss Carmen, it would be useless to waste your energy." The voice was deep and scary; it sent chills down her spine. Carmen looked around but didn't see anybody, until she noticed something in the corner, moving, then he appeared. Carmen stared at him, almost identical to her father, but his face was severally burnt.

"What do you what? Why am I here?" "Carmen, allow me to introduce myself. I am Matt Veach, your fathers bother. And you my dear are the next heir to the Tipo Castle." Carmen kept her gaze on him. "Well, that's one way to make an entrance." Matt glared at her eyes glowing red still.

"Do not be a little smart ass with me!" Carmen still watched his every move. "So, what do you want Matt?" Matt faced Carmen stood in front of her. "Well, that depends." "On what?" "On you Carmen. Has anybody ever explained to you what I am considered?" "A rouge." "Well, that's one way to put it but no. I am the next generation of lycans. You see, a lycan can only be born from having lycan blood within its parents. However me, well once when you eat, or should I say bite a human, they transform. They can be turned into a lycan, a natural rouge."

"So, Matt, what does that have to do with me?" Carmen asked, not sure if she really wanted the answer, but right now she didn't really have a choice. She swallowed hard and continued to keep her gaze on Matt.

Matt laughed an evil chuckle that sent chills down Carmen's body. "Since you are already a natural born lycan, but didn't have the chance to change, if I bite you, you will be very powerful, very strong. You can rule, with me, we will be in control of the clans." Carmen looked at him in disgust. "And why the fuck would I do that?" "Because Carmen, without me, you will never be able to change, you will be nothing but a simple little guardian." Carmen looked down, then looked back up at Matt, eyes glowing green. "No." Matt's eyes grew redder. "Then you and your whole family will die Carmen." Matt vanished right in front of Carmen's eyes, she sat there, scared, alone, and helpless.

"We have to find her before he hurts her Mark!" Chris was standing in front of Marcus. "Chris, he could be anywhere. What do you propose we do?" Chris knew Marcus was right. Chris couldn't stand being here not doing anything when his daughter was out there somewhere, with a monster. He went outside for fresh air and to think, while everybody else was talking about trying to find Carmen. Chris sat down on the stairs. Ian followed him outside and sat down next to him. Neither said anything, they just sat there. "Mr. Goshen, we're not going to be able to find her, are we?" Ian looked at Chris, who was starting to cry. "Ian, I don't know. He wants something, but now I don't know what. I don't know what to do." They sat there for a minute before Chris spoke again. "Ian, do you love her?" Ian didn't even have to think about the answer. "Yes, yes sir I do." Chris nodded and started to cry again. Ian put his hand on Chris's shoulder, trying to comfort him.

"Well, well, well, are we crying?" The voice startled both Chris and Ian but when they looked up, they both immediately stood up. Matt stood there in front of them. "Where's my daughter Matt? Where is she?!" "Wow, calm down brother, and you better listen to me if you ever want to see her alive again." Chris backed away from him, allowing Matt to continue. "Here's the deal Chris. You, your family and everybody else, including little Romeo there, will leave by tomorrow night. And I will take over the clans." "And if we don't?" "Simple, I bite your little Carmen, she turns rouge, and I still kill you." Chris started to walk towards Matt until Ian stopped him. "See that's the sprit brother. Get mad, get angry." "If you touch my daughter . . ." Chris charged past Ian and ran towards Matt until he shimmered away. Chris stood where Matt stood, smelling. He could smell Carmen, but there was something else, another smell, something vaguely familiar. He stood there, praying that Matt wouldn't do her any harm. "Ian, we have to find her."

Quickly they both ran inside. Chris explained what Matt's intentions were. Marcus sat there, thinking. "So, what are we going to do Mark?" Allision asked taking a seat to him. Chris held Kate who was holding back tears. Marcus finally stood up to speak. "We will send guards to search the town, and we wait, once when he arrives tomorrow night we will be ready. If he really wants the clans, he will bring Carmen here. Once when Matt releases her, we attack. That's all we can do for now."

Marcus sent out the orders, but it didn't seem to make the matters better. Everybody just sat there, worried. Ian was pacing the floor, when Jai asked him to sit down, he snapped at her. "Mom, how can everybody just sit here and not do anything when Carmen is out there with that monster?! And look, here we are sitting around not doing a damn thing!" Ian sat down next to her, Jai held him. "Ian, listen we will find her ok son?" Ian felt disgusted, desperately not trying to cry. "Our last words, we were fighting. Mom, I didn't, I didn't get to apologize, I didn't get to hold her and tell her how much I love her." Ian fell into him mother's arms crying, and Jai held him, allowing him to let it out." "It will be ok son, we will find her." Kate started to cry as Chris held her. Everybody sat there until the morning came.

The guards finally showed up as the morning sun was rising. Marcus stood up. "Well?" One guard spoke, "I'm sorry my Lord, we searched the whole town and the woods within 15 miles of the castle and there is no sign of him or Carmen. I'm sorry." Furious Marcus picked up a chair and threw it against a wall, the chair shattering to pieces. "Search again, find her, find my granddaughter!" in fear all the guards bowed and quickly walked out the doors. "Mark." Allision started to walk towards Marcus. "Allison, don't touch me right now!" Frightened Allision stepped back. Chris got up and walked outside, Ian following him.

Chapter 6

Carmen was still tied up, her arms aching, her eyes sagging from not sleeping but she was too scared to even think about sleep. She started to hear noises around her, voices, but she couldn't tell when they were coming from. Suddenly Matt appeared, holding a plate of food. "Aww, Carmen, honey you must be hungry." Matt tried to feed Carmen a piece of bread but she kicked the plate right of Matt's hands.

He reached around and slapped her in her face. Turning around, eyes glowing green, Carmen faced him. "My father and grandfather are you to kill you, so if I was you, I would be preparing for your own funeral, burnt face." Matt smiled a flashy pair of fangs, leaning into to face her. "No honey, I will kill them, and then I'm going to kill you. Just like how I killed Leo's father, the whole council, and how I almost killed Leo, Jai and your little boyfriend." Carmen glared at him.

"You killed Leo's father?" "Yes my dear, I did. And it was a pleasure to do it." Carmen spit in Matt's face. Wiping it away, eyes glowing red like blood. "I'm going to save you for last you little bitch." Carmen's heart beat started beating faster and faster, and then he disappeared again. Carmen was wondering how he was doing that. She stopped trying to get lose and thought for a moment. If she could posse the power of earth, why not the other powers, after all her mother was the Pure White. *'How can I get loose from these ropes?'* Carmen thought to herself. "Fire would work." She said out loud.

Thinking about fire, how warm it was, Carmen closed her eyes, and felt the tingling sensation and then smelt something burning. Suddenly her arms were free. Carmen smiled. "Now time to get out of here."

Carmen walked around the room, scoping every wall she could find, following then until they came to another wall. Feeling around, Carmen felt some wood, moving her hands down she found the doors handle, wiggling it, the door didn't move. Carmen rubbed the ring Ian gave her, she knew somehow they was going to save her. Carmen returned to where she was sitting, breaking off a leg off the chair, Carmen was ready for when Matt came back.

Ian followed Chris into the woods, far away from the castle. "Mr. Goshen, where are you going?" Chris didn't answer but Ian continued to follow him, until soon they came to a clearing, and Ian saw three cabins. Chris walked up to the one in the middle and sat down on the porch.

Looking around, Ian realized these must be the cabins Chris and his father made. "You know Ian, your father proposed to Kate at first, but Kate and I had a connection, we fell madly in love, and the night she and Leo were to be married, I promised her I was going to come back for her, then my other brother, Cole, attacked us and killed Kate, it was the power of everybody that we magically healed her and brought her back. But all this time I always believe it was the power of love that brought her back to me. Then Carmen came into our lives and, I thought I would never love anybody s much as I love Kate, but Carmen, she's special, I was wrong. Kate and Carmen mean the world to me. Carmen was our miracle, she died at birth but I was able to heal her. It's all about love, Ian, everything is. I feel like I already lost Carmen." Ian looked at him, seeing the despair in his face, hearing it in his voice. "Sir, don't, don't talk like that. You are strong, and we need your strength, I need your strength. I need you to be strong, for me, please?"

Chris looked down, ashamed that Ian looked up to him like that; Chris couldn't help but feel he let everybody down. "We will find her Mr. . . ." "Ian please call me Chris." Ian swallowed. "Ok, Chris, we will find her." They sat there, just looking around, slowly it started to become darker, and they headed back to the castle.

Matt appeared in front of Carmen, scaring her. "Ok, time to party."

Carmen held up the stick. "Don't touch me or I will stab you." "Carmen let's not make this difficult." Matt walked towards Carmen and quickly she rammed the sick into his arm. "You little bitch!" Matt ran up to her and grabbed the stick and broke it in half, scared Carmen started to run, but Matt shimmered in front of her, gabbing her by her neck, slapping her face again, this time busting her lip open, blood started to run down her face. "Listen to me Carmen, if I was going to kill you I would have done it already, and honestly what do you think you were going to do with that stick?" Carmen didn't say anything. "I didn't think so. Let's go." Carmen suddenly felt dizzy and when she opened her eyes, they were in front of the castle.

Carmen pushed past Matt and ran into the castle. Marcus and Chris were standing there when she opened the door. Carmen quickly ran into Chris's arms, looking at her lip, he grew furious, but he held her tight. Matt walked up behind them. "So, what's your choice?" Immediately Matt was surrounded by guards. "Ok, well I guess we'll do it your way."

He swung around and grabbed two guards by their troughs, ripping them out. He jumped on the back of another guard and twisted his neck. The other two guards stabbed each other trying to get to Matt, but he was too fast for them. All of this happened so fast, nobody had time to react. Matt shimmered behind Marcus and threw him against the wall. Chris stood in front of Carmen, guarding her. Mat walked up to Chris, facing him. "Since you want to attack your own brother, Chris, I'll take Carmen, as a souvenir."

Ian and Leo ran behind Matt, trying to hold him back. "Kate, take Carmen out of her now!" Chris yelled as Kate grabbed Carmen and shimmered. They were in the secret room. Chris charged towards Matt, but he shimmered away. Ian and Leo falling to the floor and Chris stopping in his tracks. "Chris!!" Chris heard the yell, it was Kate, but she appeared in front of him. "Chris, Chris he took her again." Chris looked around, smelling, there was that smell again, Chris closed his eyes trying to remember where it was from. His eyes opened wide. "I know where they are at."

Chapter 7

"Let me go!" Carmen was struggling against Matt's hold on her arms. He drugged her down a flight of stairs, throwing her in a dark room, where she hit her head on the flood, busting the side of her head open, blood flowing down. The smell of blood made Matt's eyes grow even redder.

As he walked closer to her, Carmen backed away, until he cornered her, he had her scared to death. With his teeth blaring, he went to bite down on her neck until the door busted into flames. There stood Marcus, Chris, Leo, Ian and Kate. Carmen went to try to run to them until Matt grabbed her by her hair, standing behind her. "So, have we come to an agreement?" Chris glared at him. "No, I came to get my daughter back."

"I don't think you will be getting her back." Matt looked down then looked up, with his teeth blaring out, eyes glowing red like a blazing fire. Matt bit down on Carmen's shoulder, she screamed out in pain. "No!" Chris yelled out as he ran towards Matt. Matt threw Carmen, her body sliding against the floor. Ian ran up to her but she was unconscious. He picked her up and ran her up the stairs, Kate following him.

Chris charged at Matt, pushing him against a wall. Matt jumped over his head, Marcus ran towards him, Chris behind Matt and Leo on the other side of Marcus. All three were circling Matt. "Why? Why us? Why my daughter?" Chris faced him eye to eye.

"Now once when she transform, you will have to banish her, and knowing you, you will go with her. You will now know how it feels to be hated." Marcus grabbed Matt, holding him by his hands as Leo and Chris attacked him, holding him on the ground. Marcus threw a fire ball on him, catching him on fire. Chris grabbed the broken chair and broke off another piece of a leg and stabbed Matt in the chest. The three of them watched as he screamed, the smell of burnt flesh filling the room, until the screams died down, and Matt's body was nothing but a pile of smoking dust. "Carmen." Chris whispered as he quickly ran up the stairs, Leo and Marcus following him. They found Kate kneeling over Carmen's body healing the wounds on her body, including the bite mark on her shoulder. "She's not dead, but what about the bite? Has the venom spread yet?" Ian looked up at Chris, Marcus standing next to him.

"Let's get her home, maybe she will be fine, that's all we can hope for." They carried Carmen to the van, and drove back to the castle. Ian carried Carmen to her room, laying her down the bed.

Ian, Chris, and Kate never left Carmen's side, but she never woke up. Almost a month has gone by and still nothing. The day went by as the same, but night fall came Carmen tossed and turned in her, slowly she started to wake up. When she opened her eyes she saw everybody surrounding her, then they all gasped. "What, what happened?" Carmen said as she sat up rubbing her head. Kate sat down next to her, "Carmen, honey, how do you feel?" "A little dizzy and I have a major headache. But other than that, I feel fine, I feel great. Why?" "Do you remember what happened?" Carmen rubbed her head. "I, I can't remember. How long have I been asleep? And why is everybody staring at me?!" nobody answered so Carmen got up and went into the bathroom. After washing her face, she looked in the mirror. Her eyes, they used to be green, but now, now they were red. Carmen ran out of the bathroom.

"What happened to me? My eyes are red!" Kate walked over to Carmen. "Carmen, Matt bit you and then you passed out." Carmen looked at her and her eyes grew redder. "What am I?" "Everybody leave please, except Chris and Ian." Marcus, Jai, Leo and Allision left. "Carmen, you are a rouge now, but you haven't change yet, as long as you don't change you will not become an official rouge."

Carmen sank to the floor. "Carmen you haven't change yet, if you don't change tonight you will never change, you will only posse every power known to us." "Ok, I won't change." Chris walked over to her. "Carmen, it's not a choose, it's not that easy. To try not to change is very painful, it will burn, and it will feel like your scull is splitting in half. But we are all here to help you." The moon was starting to rise and Carmen was starting to sweat, panting, and her eyes started to turn even redder. Ian and Chris laid her down on her bed. Kate shut the window and locked the door.

Carmen's back started to arch as she was yelling out in pain, Ian and Chris holding her down. Carmen started to grow fangs and she grew stronger, making it harder for Ian and Chris to hold her down fully. Carmen started to scream even louder. "Chris the pain is going to kill her if she doesn't change!" Kate started to pace the floor. Carmen lead out louder, this time loud enough to ring everybody's ears, echoing through the room, then the yell turned unto a growl. "Damn it Chris! We have to let her change, she will die!" Chris looked at her, "No Kate, we only have to wait a few more hours before the moon starts to set, once when that happens, this will be over." Kate looked at him, a tear dropping down her cheek.

"Kate, get us a wet rag and a belt." Chris looked at her as she was watching Carmen, yelling, her eyes glowing an even redder color. "Now Kate!" Kate finally blinked and finally looked at Chris. She went to the bathroom and grabbed a rag and wetted it down, running out of the bathroom she threw the rag at Chris as she ran to the closet and pulled out a leather belt and walked over to the bed. "Put it in her mouth Kate."

Chris instructed. "Carmen, Carmen, honey can you hear me?" Over a scream Carmen was able to look at Kate. "Mom," "Ok Carmen, I need to put this in your mouth ok?" Carmen opened her mouth reveling long fangs; Kate stuck the belt in her mouth. "Ok Kate, take the rag and wipe her face, she is sweating bad." Carmen muffled yell still was able to ring through their ears. She arched her back one last time in pain, it took all the strength of both Chris and Ian to hold her down.

Suddenly her body went limp over their bodies. "What happened? What's wrong with her?" Kate started to pace back and forth. "Is she dead?" Chris went to remove the belt from her mouth, bite holes through the leather belt. Slowly she opened her mouth, reliving nothing but plain white teeth. Quickly he opened her eyes, also reveling green eyes. "Kate, go get some water and aspirin. Now we wait." Chris said.

Chapter 8

They sat there waiting, as Carmen slept. Marcus and Allision sat down by Carmen's bed as the local doctor checked her over, making sure there wasn't any permanent damage. The doctor soon left and there was nothing left to do but wait. There were bruises on Carmen's arms where Chris and Ian held her down. Ian sat down on the bed next to her; he brushed back her hair from her ear, leaned in and whispered in her ear. "Baby, Carmen, it's me Ian, if you're in there, I need you to wake up. I need you to come back to us. Because I want to tell you how much I love you, how much I need you, with me, in life, forever." He kissed her lips, and sat there with her, holding her hand.

Everybody waited by Carmen's bedside, hours went by and nothing, not even a move. Suddenly Carmen started to toss and turn in her bed, Ian jumped back at first, until she opened her eyes, her beautiful green eyes. "Baby?" She looked over at Ian. "Ian?" He held her in his arms.

Chris and Kate ran over to Carmen. "Honey are you ok?" Kate rubbed Carmen's head. "My arms hurt." Kate laughed as she held Carmen in her arms. That afternoon after Carmen took a shower, everybody ate lunch together, as a family. Chris watched as Ian and Carmen held hands and walked in the garden. "They are in love, aren't they Chris?" Chris turned around to see Marcus. "Yes sir, almost . . ." "Almost like you and Kate were." "We are still in love sir, when I look at her I still feel like a teenager.

Marcus looked down. "If I would of known the way the way you felt about her, it would have been you picked first, I want you to know that Chris." "Thank you Mark." Chris left the room as Marcus stayed back and watched as s Ian picked up Carmen and swung her around. Marcus laughed as they fell on the ground, laughing and rolling in the grass. Suddenly Marcus got an idea. He went down stairs and asked that the Taylors' and Goshen's to be asked to come to the library.

"A ball?" Jai asked confused. "No, no, more like a party. Just like Kate had." Marcus explained. "But for what? We already know who he will choose." Chris stated. "Well, we cannot make it official with allow the clans to know. So what do you think?" Everybody looked at each other, and then started talking all at once. All day they stayed together planning the party, trying to make sure it was going to be perfect. That night Chris and Leo surprised Ian about the party, and he excitedly agreed.

The following night Kate took Carmen to the cabins as everybody else was getting the party finals ready. "Mom, what are we doing here?" "Well, there's something I want to give you. And it's in here." Kate opened the door, and that's when Carmen realized this was the cabin, the cabin she born in. Her mother came down the stairs carrying a white box. Carmen sat down on the couch, as Kate sat down next to her. She opened the box slowly reveling a wonderful jade green dress. "This is the dress I wore at my wedding, and I would love for you to have it Carmen." "Mom, it's beautiful, but why are you giving this to me?" Kate smiled "Let's just say it's a surprise." Carmen smiled back. "Mom, it would be an honor to have this dress, thank you." Carmen hugged her mother. "Come on Carmen, let's get you dressed." After getting dressed Carmen and Kate walked back to the castle.

As they entered the doors, she saw Jai, Leo, Marcus, and Allision, and her father all standing together. Marcus stepped up to speak, "May I present Mr. Ian Taylors." Everybody turned to Marcus who moved away and behind him was Ian, dressed in a black suit with a green tie. "Mr. Taylors, it is time for you to choose your wife." Smiling Ian walked over to Carmen. He got down on one knee, "Miss Carmen Goshen, will you do me the honors of becoming my wife?" Smiling and crying at the same time, Carmen said, "Yes, of course I will." Ian got up and faced Carmen. "Tonight? Right now Carmen?" Eyes wide

Carmen replied, "Now?" "Yes, your grandfather has agreed to marry us, tonight, if you wish." Carmen looked at Ian, "I wouldn't have it any other way, Ian." He smiled and took Carmen by her hand and led her in front of Marcus. "By the power of the Tipo Clan, and the acceptance of the remaining clans, I now pronounce you Mr. and Mrs. Ian Taylors. You may now . . ." Without Marcus finishing, Ian grabbed Carmen by her faced and kissed her. Holding her hands up, Carmen made white roses fall around them.

THE END